GREENMONKEYGAMEBOOKS

PRESENTS

THE FALL OF DISTRICT-U

A PICK YOUR PATH ADVENTURE

Also by Matt Beighton

Poetry
Tig You're It: And other poems from the playground

The Shadowland Chronicles
The Spyglass And The Cherry Tree
The Shadowed Eye

Monstacademy Series
(Ages 7+)
The Halloween Parade
The Egyptian Treasure
The Grand High Monster
The Machu Picchu Mystery
The Magic Knight

Pick Your Path Series
Escape From Sherwood
Desolate Tomb
Beast of London
The Fall Of District-U

CHOOSE CAREFULLY...

THE FALL OF DISTRICT-U

Printed in the United Kingdom

First printed 2023

A CIP catalogue record for this book is available from the British Library.

ISBN: 978-1-915814-00-5

illustrated by Darwin Setiawan

cover illustration by Darwin Setiawan

www.mattbeighton.co.uk

www.pickyourpathadventures.com

"Your future is whatever you make it.

So make it a good one!"

- "Doc" Brown

INTRODUCTION

This is an adventure with a difference. You control the direction that the story takes. It is possible, with a few wise choices, to navigate the book with minimal risk. However, most adventurers will find that they encounter a host of pitfalls and monsters throughout their journey. How you handle these events will have consequences further on in the story. Choose wisely, and watch where you step.

CREATING YOUR CHARACTER

Before you begin your adventure, you need to generate some characteristics for your character. These are your **HEALTH** and your **STRENGTH**. These will be vital throughout your adventure. Your health will change throughout, whereas your strength will only change when you find potions or weapons that allow it to change.

To generate your **HEALTH**, roll 2 dice. Add 6 to the total. This is your original **HEALTH**. No matter what potions you find, your **HEALTH** can never go above this number.

To generate your **STRENGTH**, roll 1 die. Add 6 to the total. This is your original **STRENGTH**. Certain potions and weapons can increase your strength above this number for a short period.

FIGHTING BATTLES

When you are faced with a battle, you must defeat the enemy to move forwards in the story.

First, record the enemy's strength and health on your **BATTLE SHEET**.

1. Roll both dice and add the total to your strength. For instance, if you roll a 3 and a 5 and your strength is 9, your attack is $3 + 5 + 9 = 17$. Now do the same thing but add the strength of your foe.
2. If the scores are the same, roll again for both of you.
3. Whoever has the highest score wins this round of the battle. Remove **2 HEALTH POINTS** from the loser.
4. If you are using a special weapon, remove **1 DURABILITY** point.

If you have any ALLIES, fight for them now, repeating steps 1-4 for each ALLY.

5. Repeat steps 1-4 until the health of either you or your enemy reaches zero.
6. When one of the health scores reaches

zero, the battle is over. If your health
has dropped to zero, you have been
killed, and your adventure is over.

TESTING YOUR STRENGTH

At various points in your adventure, you
may be required to test your strength. This
is a way of testing whether you are strong
enough to complete a certain action. To test
your strength, roll two dice and add the
scores together. If the number is less than
your current strength, you are successful.
If the score is the same as or higher than
your current strength, you are unsuccessful.
You must follow the instructions each time,
depending on what you roll.

POTIONS AND ELIXIRS

During your adventure, you may be given
potions or elixirs. These have positive
effects on your health and strength. Unless
they say otherwise, **HEALTH POTIONS**
only restore your health to your original
level. Therefore, it is important to use
them wisely. **STRENGTH POTIONS** increase
your strength temporarily. Once you have
completed an action or finished a battle,
your strength returns to its original level.

Some potions restore your health fully. Others only restore a certain amount of points. These will be indicated with brackets in the name: for example, a **HEALTH POTION (+4)** will restore 4 health points. It is even more important to use these wisely. If you use a **+4 HEALTH POTION** when you are only 2 points below your maximum, you will only benefit from +2 points. The other two are wasted.

WEAPONS

Various weapons are scattered throughout the adventure. Unfortunately, they are all well-used and won't last for very long. Each weapon has a **DURABILITY**. This tells you how many rounds of battle it will last. **Note**: this isn't how many full battles, but how many individual rounds. Therefore, it is very important to use special weapons sparingly. If you are up against a weaker enemy, it's probably best to stick with your trusty sword than waste a special weapon. You can use special weapons for single rounds if you prefer; maybe you need to deliver a killer blow during a particularly close fight and only want to use 1 durability point on a weapon.

You start the adventure with a **PLASMA PISTOL**, which will last forever but doesn't have any special effects. This is to fall back on when you have no other weapons.

Some weapons may have dual effects. For instance, a **BLADE OF DEFENCE** will offer some protection during a fight and mean you only lose 1 health point per round that you lose. However, it is also very heavy and means you take a *-2 STRENGTH* hit. Remember, these benefits and negatives only affect you during rounds where you use that particular weapon. Your strength returns to normal when you use another weapon.

Various weapons may have **KEYWORDS** associated with them. If they do, make a note of them as they may give you extra benefits in certain situation.

If you run out of **WEAPON** slots, you must drop a weapon before you can take another.

ALLIES

At certain points in your adventure, you may meet others who wish to join your cause. These are classed as **ALLIES**, and you will be told when you may add them to this list. **ALLIES** are a great way to boost your fighting capabilities. After you have rolled for yourself and your enemy, you get to do the same thing again for each of your **ALLIES**.

When you meet **ALLIES**, you will be given their **STRENGTH** and **HEALTH** to record on your **BATTLE SHEET**. Sometimes, you will be asked to generate one or both of these scores. Instructions on how to do this will be given each time.

If, at any point, an **ALLY's HEALTH** drops to zero, that **ALLY** dies and cannot be used again. You may use any potions that you possess on an **ALLY**, but remember to remove them from your **PACK** when you do. You cannot split potions. Likewise, any weapons that you possess may be used by your allies. Remember to keep track of how many times they are used, the same as if you were using them yourself.

If your own health drops to zero, your adventure is over regardless of how many **ALLIES** you have. You cannot continue your quest as an **ALLY**.

You may have multiple **ALLIES** at once.

ERRATA

Fixes for any known issues can be found at mattbeighton.co.uk/errata

UPGRADES

Unlike previous Pick Your Path Adventures, this book is set in the distant future, in a time when technology has advanced to the point that your human body is merely a shell. Throughout your time in District-U, you might find ways to modify your body with powerful mech upgrades. These are often expensive but come with a range of benefits.

If you choose to purchase an upgrade, mark it off on your **BATTLE SHEET** and include any notes about how it will benefit you. Don't forget to use them during your adventure.

BACKGROUND

A thousand years in the future, Earth as we know it is a memory, a myth told to children to remind them of things that were once alive. Humans have long left the dead planet behind. Wherever they've travelled, they've wrought destruction and left scarred worlds in their wake. In this grim future, to be human is to be seen as a virus. Those that have survived have assimilated into the other races that populate the galaxy. Known as the Wide, this broad galactic system is the canvas for some of the worst battles in history. They rode aboard enormous habitats known as World Ships. These sustained them for a while, but resources soon dwindled and a sickness spread.

As humanity spread like a virus, a tyrant known only as the Emperor began his own quest for galactic domination. He began to build a vast army of loyal soldiers, recruited from every race and trained in brutal, cold warfare.

Peace was fragile and on a knife edge. It may well have lasted, but the discovery of **FLUX** in the Earth year 2985 changed everything.

This invisible force flows through the universe and is the seat of all power. The Flux Route became the most lucrative and most feared passageway in the whole of the Wide. Vast energy ships sprawled across the interstellar void trading flux and other less savoury goods.

Wherever the Emperor's armies settled on the pock-marked planets, factory systems sprung up. These sprawling, nest-like cities rose like fungus wherever flux was found.

District-Utopia was the first of its kind, designed to be perfect in every way: a utopia for its workers. But greed drove everything, and the great experiment ended with its destruction in 2988, leaving only the factory belching out fumes. Workers still poured into the district, slums emerged on the outskirts, and a black market arose.

Now, the districts are dens of despair, fit to house only scavengers and criminals. Clans rise and fall, leaving nothing but misery and a smudge on the concrete. Only one clan thrives in every district: the Imperialists. Whilst it presents itself as an independent clan, it is rumoured that they are secretly funded by the Emperor as his own private security in the slums.

All districts are led by a warlord, and Magron Thundergill rules over District-U with a plasma fist. It was he who destroyed your family. It was he who drove you from the district as a child. It is he who you have come back for...

YOUR CHARACTER'S NAME:

Starting strength:
Current strength:

Starting health:
Current health:

WEAPONS:

Weapon:
Strength effect:
Durability:
Notes:

Weapon:
Strength effect:
Durability:
Notes:

Weapon:
Strength effect:
Durability:
Notes:

Weapon:
Strength effect:
Durability:
Notes:

Weapon:
Strength effect:
Durability:
Notes:

Weapon:
Strength effect:
Durability:
Notes:

Weapon:
Strength effect:
Durability:
Notes:

Weapon:
Strength effect:
Durability:
Notes:

Weapon:
Strength effect:
Durability:
Notes:

ALLIES:

Name:
Strength:
Health:
Notes:

Name:
Strength:
Health:
Notes:

Name:
Strength:
Health:
Notes:

BATTLES:

Enemy: Strength: Health:	Enemy: Strength: Health:	Enemy: Strength: Health:
Enemy: Strength: Health:	Enemy: Strength: Health:	Enemy: Strength: Health:
Enemy: Strength: Health:	Enemy: Strength: Health:	Enemy: Strength: Health:
Enemy: Strength: Health:	Enemy: Strength: Health:	Enemy: Strength: Health:

YOUR PACK:

Download and print

mattbeighton.co.uk/media

MECH UPGRADES

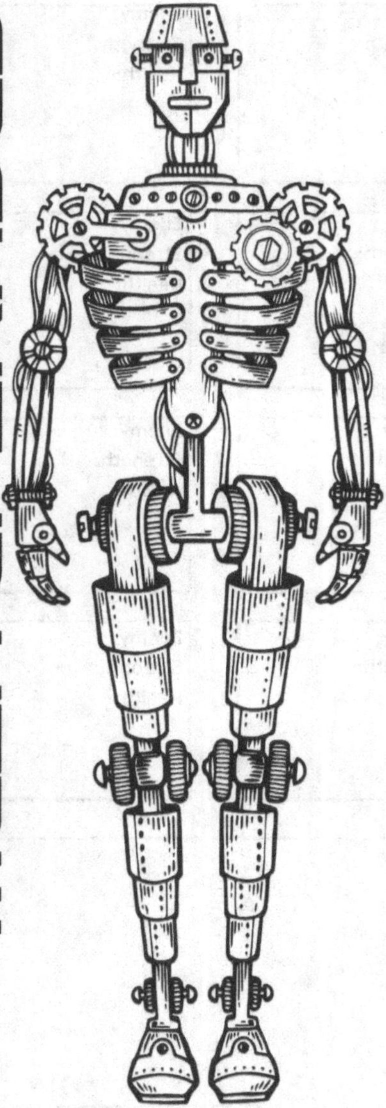

- ☐ **NIGHT VISION**
- ☐ **SILVER-TONGUE MICROCHIP**
- ☐ **MECHHEART IMPLANT**
- ☐ **POWER GAUNTLET**
- ☐ **SKELETAL STRENGTHENING**
- ☐ **PISTON LEGS**
- ☐ **SPIKED FEET**

TOXICITY LEVEL:

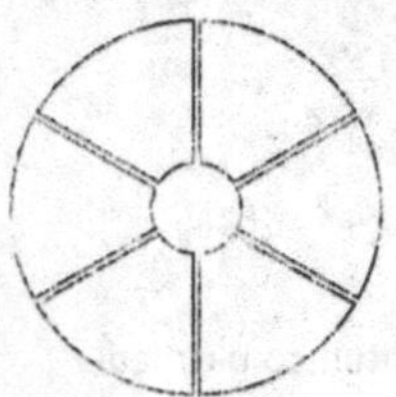

Keep track of your toxicity level.

Once all of the sections are filled in, you will lose **2 HEALTH POINTS** each time you turn to a new section until you reach fresh air or perish.

You stand at the gateway to District-U,
a sprawling mass of energy, slums and
broken dreams. It may not be the biggest
district in the Wide, but it has a well-
earned reputation as the most dangerous.
At the last census, there were three million
bodies living within the rusted steel walls
of the city, and pretty much all of them are
scraping a living buying, selling and stealing
the things that everyone else wants.

When the district was first built, it was
supposed to be the start of a utopian
future. It was the prototype for everything
that followed, hence the name: District-
Utopia. It didn't take long to realise that
it was never going to live up to its name.
Nowadays, only those who live on the top
levels still call it that. The flux factories in
the middle of each district were designed to
provide jobs for the bodies that flocked to
live near them, but artificial flux-minds and
metronomic androids soon replaced them
all. The mines still pump out flux; only now,
nobody benefits but the owners.

It's been a long time since you were last

here; it feels like more than one lifetime ago that you managed to escape the glare of Magron Thundergill and his legions of guards. There's unfinished business there, but your own revenge will have to wait. There are other things on your mind as you pick your way through the slums and begin to head towards the nest of alleyways that surround the central flux core at the heart of the district.

Overhead, you hear the continuous drumbeat of rain against the steel rooftops, but none of it reaches down to your level. Amongst the slums and shantytowns of the downtrodden criminal class, not even sunlight dares to show its face. The flickering electric lights and buzzing neon signs are all that fight against the grim darkness.

You pull your trench coat tighter and stuff your hands into your pockets. Your fingers close around your **PLASMA PISTOL**, the only weapon you've managed to get your hands on, and your wallet stuffed with notes to the sum of 300 **DING**. It's not much, but it might get you a coffee in one of the back-alley shacks that are hawking their trade out of every other window.

You've been given a name and a place to find work. Mandrake and the Rusty Pipe. Mandrake is a rising star amongst a loose group of anarchists from a range of clans. They've realised that working together is the best way to get rid of people like Thundergill, and they are always looking for outside help. Finding the Rusty Pipe bar has to be your first goal. Speak to Mandrake and see what he has to offer. After that, all bets are off.

Wherever you look, you see a familiar line up of villainy and desperation that you know are your equals. Humans have been shunned in the factories for as long as you can remember as a direct result of their greed and their assault on the Wide. Down here, nobody cares what you look like, just what you have that's worth stealing. Strange and dark creatures of all descriptions shuffle past, staring at you and measuring you up. It wouldn't be a wise move to stand around looking like a tourist for much longer.

Every building is covered in faded posters, sheet steal and the hyper-rich colours of clan graffiti. Your own clan, the Steel Fists, is long gone, but some of the others have held on. You spot the laughing mask of the Jongleurs, the steel-clenched fist of the Mechist Guild and, of course, the lightning bolt of the Imperialists. The war to control the streets has been waged for centuries, but few clans cling on for long. Unless they have big money behind them, of course. The Imperialists have long been the unofficial guards of the Emperor. His reach extends to nearly every corner of the galaxy, and there's a clan of Imperialists in every District. They are strong, well-funded and fearless.

Other than that, there are the Virulants. Not so much a clan as a group of diseased and infected lost souls, the Virulants rarely leave the pits below the district. When they do, they are a constant reminder of the dangers of getting too close to flux.

Eager to step out of the pool of neon light, you glance around you. New people flood the District daily, and shacks rise and fall as quickly. The streets you knew as a child are long gone, and the ones in front of you will probably be different tomorrow. The inner wall that surrounds the toughest streets towers over you, perhaps a few hundred yards ahead. There are a hundred different passages snaking away, but only two seem to head towards the wall. Straight ahead, the alley seems to continue in a straight line towards an entrance gate. From here, you can see that it is loosely guarded. To your right, the alleyway is dark and narrow, but a steady flow of foot traffic is moving in both directions.

To head straight on, turn to **17**.

To take the dark alleyway to your right, turn to **279**.

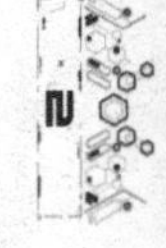

2

You cautiously descend into the darkness, feeling your way along the damp wall, desperately searching for a switch or other source of light. Along the wall, random sparks of electricity leap from broken wires. The darkness draws you in, shrouding you in its inky blackness as soon as you are a few paces from the steps. You glance back over your shoulder, but there is no light there, either. You begin to curse yourself for closing the door behind you but quickly realise that you left it ajar. Something else has closed it, something that is down here in the tunnel with you.

Turn to **39**.

3

The steps are steep and unforgiving. By the time you approach the doorway, your lungs are burning, and you are forced to lean against the wall for a moment to regain your breath. As you press your head against the metal, you hear a solitary voice ranting and raving inside the room. You press harder, trying to make out what they are saying, but it is nothing but a muffled mess. You are convinced that the only person still remaining in the core is Thundergill, but you have no way of knowing what he is up to in there or if he is armed.

To knock on the door and call out to Thundergill, turn to **150**.

To storm in, armed and ready to fight, turn to **167**.

4

When you finally wake, you push your elbows against the hard bed beneath, desperate to prop yourself up. Your chest feels like it's being opened up again by the flux pulse, so you slump back and whimper.

"I've had my men sew you up," Mandrake says from somewhere in the room. "I do wish you hadn't been so violent with them. It's hard to find good henchmen in these parts. Cheap ones, at least."

You mumble something about them opening your chest like a zipper, but Mandrake laughs it away as though it's nothing. "You'll be fine in a few hours. You men are such babies. The stimshot kept you alive, and my people have done the rest. It'll hurt for a long time, and there'll be a lovely scar, but you'll be back on your feet and working for me in no time. I'll make sure you make it up to me."

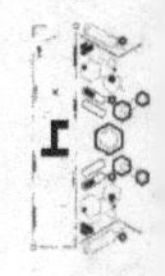

The thought of ever moving again makes you feel sick. Even lying still, the pain blossoms in your chest with every pulsing beat of your heart. As if reading your mind, Mandrake continues to talk. "You've heard of a broken heart, yes? Yours was very broken. Shattered, in fact. We took care of it. No charge, of course."

Mandrake goes on to explain that you have been fitted with a **MECHHEART**. It is a high-quality piece of equipment and isn't likely to fail any time soon. It increases your base **STRENGTH** by 1.

"I will leave you to rest up," she says, laughing, and you hear the door shut behind her.

You rest for a few hours before you feel able to rise. You roll out of bed and find your clothes and weapons in a box in the corner of the small room. There's a **GET-WELL** card with your name and a photo of your sleeping face printed on the front. Somebody, you assume Mandrake, has scrawled a note next to it: "You owe me". Add **GET-WELL CARD** to your **PACK**.

You throw on your clothes before stepping through the only door. It leads out onto the mezzanine floor, which skirts the walls of the tower. Below you, you can see the bloodstained concrete where your fight took place. Above you, there seems to be another mezzanine; however, the second floor only clings to one wall.

To your right is the staircase back down to the ground floor. You get the sense that it would be a bad idea to continue exploring down there. Taking care not to make too much noise on the metal grating, you edge around the floor until you reach another room. This one seems to hang on the outside of the tower wall like a bird's nest, with the doorway cut through the concrete itself. You glance inside and see a heavy piece of weaponry resting against the far wall. From where you are standing, it looks like a **NECTROTIC FLUX CANON**. They use a modified mixture of flux energy and irradiated waste to produce a chemical that strips the flesh from the bones of anything hit by it. You've heard about them, everybody has, but nobody you know has ever seen one.

The room itself is small, and the floor looks rotten. Even from the doorway, you can feel a draft floating up through the gaps.

You can enter the room to pick up the

canon by turning to **247**.

If you'd sooner leave it alone and continue further along the walkway, turn to **141**.

Out in the open of the wider avenue, you get a better look at the different levels of the district. Down here on the street, with the rivers of rain and waste water running in channels down the road, the buildings are illuminated by strip lights and neon tubes. In these slums, you can buy anything and anyone. Glass storefronts show off their wares, and street hawkers dance their dance outside each door, promising you salvation on the other side. You push them aside and make your way slowly amongst the crowds. You pull your hood tighter around your face, but you needn't worry. Nobody gives you a second glance; you're one more lost face in a sea of anonymity.

Here and there are signs of the utopia that the districts once aimed to be. Long-abandoned arcades, filled with flickering, noisy games, hypno-machines and flux-portals sit empty between high-rise piles of steel and sheet metal. The odd skycar zips through the air high above, but since they became a sign of the ultra-wealthy, most of the high-ups prefer to move about discreetly.

Life in the district doesn't just happen at ground level. Steel platforms and concrete walkways crisscross the wide road at every level, providing walkways and roads for those who are able to afford the more luxurious slums higher up. There is no true luxury in the district, not even on the highest level where the sun still dares to bare its face once in a while. Just less discomfort. You duck into the shadows created by an overhang at the sound of a drone flitting through the sky. It doesn't seem to be doing anything more malicious than making a delivery, but you are hard-wired to avoid the damned things. They weren't always so innocent.

As you progress along the road, you reach a set of steel steps, rusted and edged with faded yellow stripes, that leads up to the next level of the slum. You never dared rise that high as a kid, not even when your clan was it full strength, but the temptation is strong now. To climb the steps, turn to **281**. To continue along the street, turn to **262**.

6

Almost as soon as your body is clear of the doors, they hiss shut behind you and the carriage races out of the station. The magno-tech design pushes the vehicle forward at a tremendous speed, but you barely feel a jolt underfoot. Outside the window, the city passes by in a blur of neon light. Seen like this, you can't help but find it beautiful, almost peaceful. Only the occasional flash of light and echoing crack of gunfire shatters your wishful thinking.

Around you, graffiti and posters plaster the once-polished walls of the carriage. There are the familiar anarchist signs dotted with clan icons. In places, you can see where somebody has tried to scrub them out, as though erasing their symbols will get rid of the clans themselves. You've been part of that world; you know that they are just like mushrooms. It doesn't matter how many you destroy; when everything is as rotten as District-U, fungi will flourish.

Suddenly, the world around you slows down

as though everything is moving through thick oil. The world outside is still blurred with speed, but time has ground to a halt. You try to move, but your own limbs feel heavy and weighed down. Glancing up, you catch sight of a strange figure, balanced on top of a thin, towering pylon nestled amongst the high-rise hab units. They're wearing a hooded cloak that casts their face in a dark shadow, their hands outstretched towards you.

Bile rises in your throat, your stomach twisting into knots. It's an esper and a powerful one judging by how it has managed to warp time. You remember the warning you were given to avoid enclosed spaces until the espers had been dealt with. *Too late now*, you realise as you feel the air inside the carriage being compressed and your muscles twisted by your attacker's superior ESP powers. You gasp for breath, clawing at the window, desperate to find a catch. Every movement feels like forcing your way through steel, and there are no clasps to be found. Excited stars pinwheel across your vision, obscuring your sight while you frantically search for something heavy to smash through the glass, but you know that it's hopeless. You collapse to the

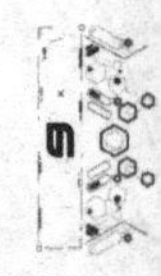

floor, your muscles wrenched from your bones, the pain slowly coursing through your body.

You can see the reflection of the esper in the polished chrome of a service hatch on the wall, and you watch them lower their hands. As soon as they do, time floods back, along with the agonising pain. You cry out and shudder, a last twitch of energy before your broken body falls silent, nothing more than a shell on an endless journey along the tramline.

7

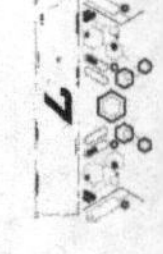

Making your way through the dense crowd, you can't help but consider your decision once more. Your heart races at the thought of showing off your prowess in the pit, but the sensible part of you knows that you are in a rush, that revenge over Thundergill won't come down here in the sweat and blood. Before you can back out, you've reached the disfigured brute of a man that is taking names. You offer him yours and are quickly escorted to a stinking room underneath the crowd. Even through the thick concrete, you can hear the pulsing beat of their roars.

The man explains that it costs 50 **_DING_** to enter each fight. "To make sure we can clean up after you," he says with a horrible sneer. "You can have the first one for free, 'cos I'm nice. If you win," he continues, his broken nose whistling as he speaks, "you'll get 250 **_DING_** as prize money. Can't say fairer than that."

If you win a fight, you are free to put your name down for further fights so long as you have enough **_DING_** to pay. You must remove the 50 **_DING_** from your pack before each fight. A fight ends when either you or your enemy are reduced to **_2 HEALTH POINTS_** or fewer. Nobody needs to die in the pit tonight.

Each opponent is selected randomly from the crowd. Roll a die and consult the table at the back of the book to see who you will fight each time. Some are stronger than others, but there are no re-rolls in the fighting pit!

Once you have had enough, can't afford any more fights or have been reduced to **_2 HEALTH POINTS_**, you must leave the fighting pit and return to the street by turning to **36**.

8

Immediately, you begin to choke on the noxious fumes that fill the sewer into which you have descended. If you have a **NIGHT VISION** mech upgrade and are able to use it successfully, turn to **205**.

If not, turn to **136**.

9

You leave the celebration behind and follow another dark alley that seems to head towards the walls of the district. As you get closer, the towering shanty buildings get taller. Each house was built as it was needed and wherever there was space. Many hang over the rooms below them, teetering inwards where the metal has rusted through, or there wasn't enough support to begin with. They give the strange sensation of walking through a tunnel, but one that has grown organically. Despite the rain, the air is hot and thick with strange aromas. You can pick out the scent of spices and oil but, over it all, wafts the unmistakable stench of flux. It doesn't matter how far you run, it never leaves you. Turn to **108**.

You break like a coward and reveal everything that you know. You mention that you are heading for the Rusty Pipe and that you are hoping to join Mandrake's rebellion. The woman seems to be taken aback at first, perhaps at the speed with which your resolve crumbled. Once you have finished, she steps closer and pats you on the head patronisingly.

"There," she says soothingly, "was that so bad? Now we can bring about a swift end to this rebellion before they recruit any more unfortunate rats to help them. In a way, you've saved hundreds of lives. Not theirs, of course, but others who might have fallen for their cause. I suppose that might sooth your ragged conscience when you try to sleep." She explodes into another fit of giggles before unlocking the cuffs around your wrists.

You follow her along a series of dark corridors until you reach a fire escape. She pushes against the bar, and you recoil in the neon lights that flood the street outside. As you step forward to leave, she lays an arm across your chest.

"I suppose you should know that we managed to get a message to Mandrake about your capture and that you might be helping us. Good luck."

The woman removes her arm, and you step through the door. Sure enough, a group of heavily-armed street soldiers are waiting in the alleyway, cloaked by the shadows of the towering factories that surround you all. Only the flickering light of the neon advertising boards, high overhead, and the sound of traffic passing over the air bridges reaches into the pool of darkness.

Before you can utter a word, they break towards you, first slowly, then at a sprint, and descend on you in a flurry of batons and blades. Betrayal isn't tolerated in the slums of District-U, something that you knew but seemingly forgot. Whether you will learn your lesson this time isn't something that Mandrake's soldiers will leave to chance; whatever remains of you will likely never be found. The meat market is always looking for fresh produce, after all.

11

You feel a fizz at the back of your brain as the chip fires up successfully, and you instantly know that it doesn't matter what you say; the guard will agree to it. You ask him to let you pass and warn him not to allow anyone else to follow you. He nods in mindless agreement.

Turn to **208**.

12

The small wretch moves back and forth in front of you, always sure to keep himself between you and the doorway. He slips his hand into his leather tunic and withdraws a thin blade. It looks sharp and well-maintained, and he moves with a swiftness that is shocking. As he stares into your eyes, he reaches out and flicks a small switch. The light fades. He kicks the door shut with his heel, and you are plunged into darkness. If you have a Night Vision mech upgrade, then you may try to enable it now. If you are successful, you suffer no negative consequences for the battle. If you don't have such an upgrade, or it fails to activate, then you are forced to fight blind. Your only

hope will be to react to any attacks that the guard makes. As such, any damage you inflict will be reduced to *1 HEALTH POINT* at a time.

WRETCHED GUARD:

Strength: 7
Health: 6

If you manage to kill the guard, you are able to fumble your way to the door, which remains unlocked. You open it and exit the cell. Turn to **145**.

13

You flex your fingers before reaching out to snatch the badge. Just as you are an inch away, the guard's eyes flash open, and he stares into your own. You freeze, hoping that he'll somehow not see you. For a second, it looks like his brain is working away, but he closes his eyes, rolls in his chair and begins to snore. You take this as a warning not to push your luck. You are confident enough to look at the rest of the room, so turn to **31**.

14

The crates echo with a hollow rining when you hit them with the butt of your pistol. You try to lift the ones at the top of the pile, but they are too heavy or have rusted together. When you try to push against them, the side crumbles, and your arm plunges through up to your elbow. Something hot and sticky drips onto the back of your hand. You recoil and pull it clear, gagging at the wretched stench of death emanating from the black ooze flowing slowly up your arm. Turn to **194**.

15

The sound of gunfire explodes somewhere in the alleyway below the open window, but the woman seems uninterested. You take a seat in the small chair, noticing the mouldy padding erupting from the split leather. The armrests are damp and sticky, so you place your hands on your knees and await further instruction. As you wait, the woman grabs a rusty drill from somewhere under the table and goes to work on whatever is lying on top. Suddenly, you see a foot twitch underneath a grimy sheet and realise that she is operating on somebody. Bile rises in your throat, and you wonder what you have wandered into. Other than heading into the gunfire on the other side of the window, there doesn't seem to be any escape, so you sit tight and wait. Turn to **33**.

16

Even in this alleyway, hidden between the towering walls of factories and the metal structures that house the shops, homes and slums of the masses, the noises of the city are as loud as ever. You duck at the sound of a siren screaming through the air, but it's just another clan war screeching overhead. Occasional bits of debris clatter to the concrete blasted from sky-bikes overhead. There are no shop signs back here, so the only light arrives second-hand, weak and flickering, from the higher levels. It's just about enough to see by, but you walk with caution.

After a while, an even narrower back-alley breaks off on your left. The main passage continues straight ahead. To duck into the narrow space, turn to **29**. To continue straight ahead, turn to **77**.

You walk swiftly along the narrow street, stepping over puddles of unknown origin and dodging the cloying grasp of small children and beggars. You grip your pistol and wallet tightly and try your best not to draw attention to yourself.

It doesn't take long to reach the gate, and your initial impression was correct. There are two grunts guarding the gate, but they are more interested in wrestling each other than stopping you from entering the district. After all, what's one more body amongst thousands?

Head buried in your tall collar, you hurry through the gate and into the swarming hive beyond. Turn to **304**.

18

You search the bodies of the foxes for anything worth stealing but find nothing. The alleyway reveals nothing more than old trash and the odd broken bottle. Frustrated, you head back towards the warehouse. Turn to **172**.

19

Even though the guard is clearly drunk, the groan of the sheet metal door as you pull it open forces you to pause and reach for your weapon. He stirs in his chair but soon settles. There is a dim light in the room, provided by a flux lamp resting on a small card table in the middle of the floor. Around the walls, several bunkbeds reveal the purpose of the room. They are all empty, but the two chairs around the table are unfortunately filled with two burly anarchists. They rise and draw their weapons as soon as you step through the door.

"Don't do anything stupid," the taller of the two grumbles, spotting you reaching for your own weapon.

To do something stupid, turn to **24**.

To see what they do next, turn to **212**.

The barman stares at you as you unleash your most persuasive and charming argument. Whatever you say seems to work, and his face quickly softens. He motions to you to follow him to a small side room behind the bar, where he quickly closes the door. The room is only a few feet on either side and brightly lit by a flickering bare bulb hanging from the ceiling.

"You look like you are fed up with the emperor like the rest of us," he begins. You can sense the hidden question but don't offer an answer. "There's a group of us what is fed up, and we're fighting back. If you're interested in joining us, head to the old pie shop. 'Rise With Pies': that's our motto. Clever, huh? Remember, it's all about the pies."

Head swimming with information, you head back out into the bar. If you haven't already been to the quiet room at the back of the building, turn to **179**. Otherwise, you return to the street. Turn to **62**.

21

Wrenching back the cardboard, you suppress a shriek at the sight of a large rat with vivid red eyes staring back at you. Before you can react, it scrambles up the wall and disappears into a hole in the corner. Heartbeat racing, you notice an old plastic switch on the back wall that had been hidden by the pile. You flick it, and the computer hums to life.

It takes a few moments for the basic operating system to load, but there is nothing intuitive about how to use it. If you have a **PERSPEX DRIVE** in your **PACK**, turn to **315**. Otherwise, you treat the computer as a lost cause and return to the alleyway. Turn to **297**.

22

You approach the door and step onto the metal platform. You reach out and hammer the door with your fist. You feel a thump to your chest, and everything goes black.

Turn to **66**.

23

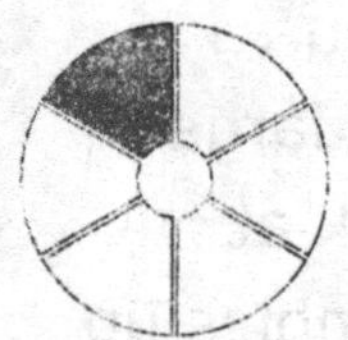 This far into the sewers, the toxic sludge flows more quickly. You push on against the tide, thankful for the greasy wooden planks that are, so far, keeping your feet dry. On occasion, you slip and grapple for a hold on the walls. You manage to keep your balance and press on until you reach another junction. The wooden structure branches off in both directions, but to the west, it ends suddenly, where it meets a metal walkway. Despite the corrosive waste that washes against it, it seems to be in good repair.

To head east, turn to **311**.

To turn west, turn to **282**.

24

Your fingers close around the hilt of your pistol at about the same time as the first pulse of flux energy hits you square in the chest. The impact of the sheet metal against your back is lost amidst the agony of the cavity that's opened up just beneath your chin. You glance down, your head swimming, and recoil at the charred edges of your own flesh. You manage to raise your pistol and fire off two pulses, one into the head of each of the anarchists. With grim satisfaction, you watch each of them slump to the floor.

Searing agony courses through your body, radiating out from your wound like the ice-cold fingers of death, but you manage to prop yourself up into a sitting position. As you edge along the wall towards the door, your hand rests on a plastic cylinder - a **STIMSHOT**. You've heard about these, the newest black-market defence against death. One shot and even the dead will come back for coffee, or so the legend goes. The cap slides off easily, and you try to find a patch of bare skin. It's not easy now that you're seeing double, but it's your only chance.

Just as you are about to stab the needle into your lower arm, the guard bursts into the room, staggering from side to side and waving a battered plasma pistol in front of his bloodshot eyes.

Turn to **250**.

25

When you look closely, you recoil in horror. There are four figures in total, each one hideously disfigured. One has no face left to speak of, their skull bare for all to see. Another is covered in puss-filled blisters that hang like empty sacks from their face. Another has a growth growing from her shoulder that looks suspiciously like a third arm terminating in a crab-like pincer. The final pestilent creature is hunched over with a twisted spine. Its face hangs loosely from its skull, and one eye is missing, leaving nothing but an empty socket. They are known throughout the districts as virulents, a race of mutants that generally live below the streets and only rise to feed or for warmth. All of the virulents are a direct result of working too closely with flux. They were once workers within the factory system, only to be cast aside worthless and disfigured when robots took over their jobs. They turn their hideous forms towards you and advance.

There's no time to scramble back over the pile of discarded crates, so you must defeat all of the creatures before you can escape.

RISE
WITH PIGS

You may fight them in any order.

SKULL-FACED MAN:

Strength: 6

Health: 5

BLISTERED MAN:

Strength: 8

Health: 6

PINCER-HANDED WOMAN:

Strength: 10

Health: 6

EYELESS MAN:

Strength: 6

Health: 7

If you manage to defeat them, turn to **215**.

26

It doesn't take long before you hear a click on the other side of the door, and a hatch swings open to reveal a steel grate and a pair of watery, bloodshot eyes. "Who are you?" the person on the other side asks. It's a different voice to the tannoy but just as on edge.

You explain who you are and that Mandrake

sent you to help them. The eyes disappear
for a moment, and you can just make out
a hurried conversation. Finally, a new set
of eyes return; these ones are sterner. The
left eye is clearly the result of a botched
black market upgrade; the pupil flickers in
and out of focus and spins slowly around
the socket. Whatever it was supposed to
do, it's a bad job. "Prove it," the new voice
demands. "What's our motto?"

Choose your answer.

"Trust in the crust!" - Turn to **273**.

"Rise With Pies!" - Turn to **45**.

"The Emperor Must Pie!" - Turn to **165**.

27

Piece by piece, your body is stripped away
and replaced with the cold metal of the
mechist's own devising. Your limbs are
seizing, and the loss of blood is beginning
to take its toll. Around you, the room spins
and blurs at the edges of your vision. The
mechist strolls over to you, casual and
calm. He reaches out with a metal hand
and grabs you underneath your chin,

pulling your face up to stare into his own. There is a dark grimace on his face; you see your own pallid flesh reflected in his polished glasses. There is little of you left to recognise, perhaps the odd scrap of skin here or there. Most of what was once you is now robotic and completely under the control of your foe.

"Welcome to the team," he whispers as his free hand moves closer to your eye. Held between the sharp pincers at the tips of his fingers, you can see the small microchip that will seal your fate. The pain as it is pushed through your pupil and past the back of your eye is excruciating, but his grip on your chin is firm. You try to blink away the pain, but your eyelid can't close over his fingers. You shudder and scream as the nanowires at the back of the chip snake out into your head and latch onto the fibres of your brain. Before you surrender complete control and your own personality is wiped by an electrical pulse, you plead in vain for your life. From here on in, you are nothing more than a tool to be used by the Mad Mechist. Your mission is over.

28

A couple of Jongleur clan members stagger past you, drunk on something or other. You momentarily recoil until your back presses against the corrugated metal of a shuttered shop front, but they pay you no attention and disappear into the night. The shop forms a corner between the main thoroughfare and a narrow side street. This one seems to be littered with discarded tech and unwanted cyborg enhancements. A handful of glass eyes twitch and spin in a sodden cardboard box, and a pile of rusting mech-limbs looks ominous in the growing gloom. On the plus side, the side street seems to be well-covered and dry. To continue along the main road, turn to **236**. To investigate the side street, turn to **292**.

29

There isn't much in the dark passage, and you quickly reach an unclimbable wall at the far end. You look around for a fire escape ladder or any other way to reach a higher level, but the walls are bare other than a few clan signs and old fliers plastered to the concrete and steel. You turn to return to the main alley but are brought up short by a mysterious hooded figure floating a few inches above the ground and between you and your escape. Turn to **318**.

30

You draw your weapon and step back further into the alley. The android flexes her neck, her simulation system kicking in to make her seem more human. There is nothing human about her glowing blue eyes or wires that twitch with every move. She doesn't seem to be armed, but her physical strength will be far superior to yours. You know your best hope is to try to dodge away from her and pick her off with shots from a distance.

SERVICE ANDROID:

Strength: 12

Health: 6

If you defeat the android, turn to **54**.

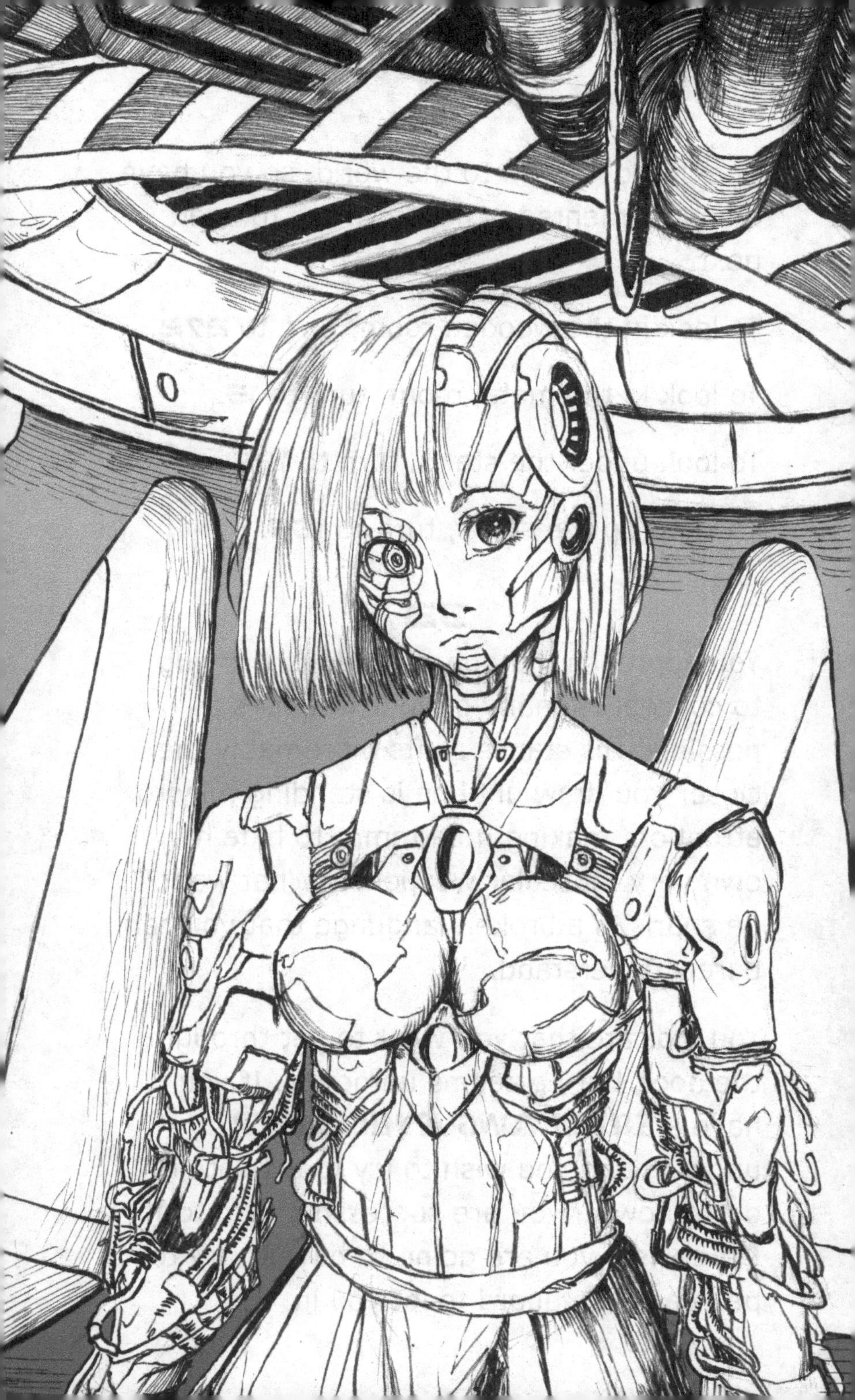

31

The guard is dead to the world, so you have a few moments to choose where to head next.

To look in the wooden room, turn to **272**.

To look in the metal room, turn to **19**.

To look under the stairs, turn to **106**.

To head up the stairs, turn to **109**.

32

You approach the guard cautiously, trying to conceal as many of your weapons as possible. His stance shifts discernably the closer you draw until he is standing fully to attention, making no attempt to hide his own very muscular weapons. "What want?" he snarls in a broken language that you can barely understand.

You indicate that you want to get through the door, but he seems unmoved. If you have a **_SILVER TONGUE MICROCHIP_** upgrade and you wish to try to activate it, do so now. If you are successful, turn to **11**. Otherwise, you are going to have to try to persuade the guard to let you in.

"What want?" he repeats as though they're the only words he knows.

You consider the type of establishment that this might be and try to give an answer that you think might work.

"I want answers!" - Turn to **113**.

"I want to fight!" - Turn to **208**.

"I want to buy some pies!" - Turn to **51**.

33

Eventually, the woman straightens up and removes two latex gloves with a snap. Wordlessly, she pushes the table through an unremarkable door into an adjoining room before returning with another. This one is empty, but you can't help but notice the dark red and brown stains, which you manage to convince yourself are rust.

"What are you here for?" she asks in an impatient but friendly voice.

You shrug your ignorance at the question, something she is clearly used to seeing. She thrusts a scratched and chipped electronic screen into your hands and waves her hand over it. It springs to life immediately, and the woman's face appears centre-screen. She looks a decade or so younger in the video but otherwise identical. She explains in short order that she is one of the best mech-operators in the district. You glance around at the dirty, filth-strewn room and have your doubts. More likely, she is a back-alley operator hoping to make a quick **DING** from cheap imports.

Turn to **103**.

34

The MindPod doesn't seem to be giving off any heat, so you move in for a closer look. The main body is black-coated metal, but there are small glass portholes punched through in a honeycomb pattern. Through them, you can see the constant flow of flux that is giving off the green luminescence. Bubbles flow past at a fantastic rate, giving you an indication of the speed and pressure held within the device. With that much flux to draw on, no wonder the espers are so powerful. There's a metal box attached to one side of the tower, which is enclosed with a solid door. A few swift hits with the butt of your pistol solves that, and it swings open to reveal a mess of wires. Mandrake didn't give you many instructions on how to destroy it, but she did mention that it needed to be rewired in a specific way to cause an explosion. If you have Pygon as an **ALLY**, turn to **246**. Otherwise, turn to **216**.

35

You try to stand, but the woman is there with a metal collar, which she swiftly fastens around your neck. You feel a jolt of electricity surge through your body, a warning of its full power. You allow the woman to lift you back onto the chair and sit, subdued. Her options to inflict pain are as limitless as your own imagination of how they will feel, and she takes her time choosing the first. As she approaches, you close your eyes and try to embrace your death, although you know that she will delay it for as long as possible. However long it takes, your end is now inevitable. Your only comforting thought is that you didn't die a traitor, betraying those who are trying to fight against the Emperor.

Nobody pays you any attention as you slink back through the crowd and out into the street. The guard on the door doesn't seem to recognise you, and you swiftly make your way along the street until you reach the main road through the district. You have approached along one branch of a crossroad.

To your right is the towering fence that surrounds the flux tower and the factory that it supports. Ahead, the road disappears into darkness, with very few people heading in that direction.

To your left, the main road heads back into the slums, and you have no desire to retrace your steps through those hives tonight.

To head towards the flux tower, turn to **131**.

To head along the dark road, turn to **290**.

Your finger rests steadily on the trigger, your eye pressed against the sight. Thundergill isn't even trying to weave or duck out of the way; his entire focus is on reaching the platform. You squeeze, and the recoil knocks you back slightly, but you keep your cheek pressed firmly against the rest.

Thundergill rocks and staggers sideways, his arm pouring blood from the fresh wound, but he's not down. He collapses forward onto the platform that rises with alarming speed. Before you can react, he is safely inside the ship, and it is rising out of the hanger and into the sky.

You drop your weapon and scream. Overhead, through the opened skydoors of the hanger, you can finally see the stars. Even they seem to be mocking your ineptitude. You had him there, in your sights, and you let him go. Mandrake will never forgive you. No doubt she'll have a bounty on your head amongst the clans. Your only worth now is to the meat-hoarders.

This isn't the ending you had in mind when you stepped through the gates of the district, but happy endings are rare in District-U. Thundergill will be back, but you

won't be here to defeat him. Your future lies
elsewhere, in a slum even more wretched
than District-U.

38

You approach the man cautiously, but he
doesn't seem intent on using the long-
barrelled weapon resting on his shoulder.
Instead, he greets you with a warm
handshake and begins to show you the
weapons on offer. None of them seems
particularly exotic, and you start to walk
away, only to find yourself dragged back
by the collar. When you turn round, intent
on showing him the error of his ways, you
are presented with something that you
have only ever dared dream of owning.
Resting on the table is an Imperialist
LIGHTNING CANON. Powered by depleted
flux and outlawed for anybody other than
the Emperor's favourite clan, you've never
even seen one. You pick it up carefully and
examine it. It seems to be in good working
order, but there's no way to know for sure.

If you wish to buy it, it will cost you 300
DING, which the grey man assures you is
a bargain. If you decide to part with your

money, add it to your **WEAPONS**. When you first decide to use this weapon, make a note of the passage you are on and turn to **178** (make a note of this number next to the weapon) to learn how to use it.

You make a hasty retreat from the stall and move as quickly as you can towards the steps, making every effort not to be noticed. Turn to **235**.

39

In the darkness, every sound seems to drill down into your soul. You find yourself jumping at every drip and clank of metal, twisting in the cool air. Tentatively, you edge along the dark tunnel, aware of the electrical wires hanging overhead. As you proceed, an eerie green glow begins to seep out of the cracks in the wall.

It takes you a moment to realise what is going on, and by then, it is too late. You are surrounded by small robotic crabs. Each one is no larger than a feral dog, but they are quick with their movements. Up close, you can see that they are made entirely of metal, painted yellow but covered in scratches. Each one has a pair of green eyes that seem to form the swirl of a galaxy as they stare at you. The sound of their metallic pincers chattering in excitement at the prospect of a meal grates against your ears like stones on glass. Other than the strange green glow of their eyes, you are going to have to fight them in the dark. For the duration of this battle, you suffer a -2 **STRENGTH** handicap.

The crabs attack one by one, dropping from the walls and springing up from your feet. Roll a die. You must defeat that number of crabs before you attempt to proceed. To move on, test your strength. If you are successful, you may leap past the crabs and continue along the tunnel. If you fail, you must reroll the die and battle that many crabs. Continue to do this until you pass a strength test or die.

ROBOTIC CRAB:
Strength: 5
Health: 4

If you are able to proceed, turn to **148**.

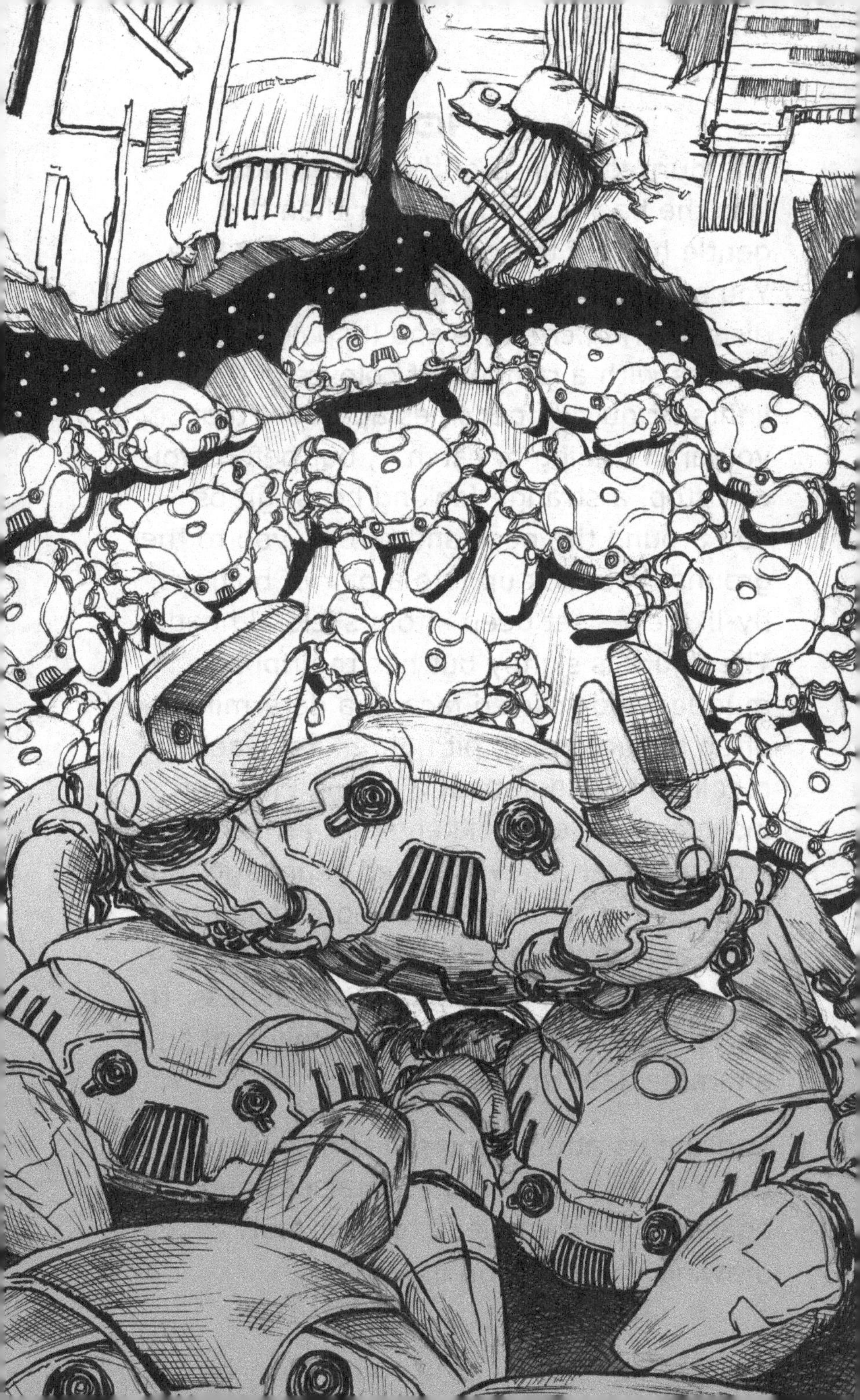

40

The hurried sounds of the street fade into the background, quieter than the gentle hum of the occasional electric bike. You are focussed entirely on the rapidly disappearing creature and its pale fur that dances with a rainbow of colours in the lights. It quickly becomes apparent that you aren't going to catch it, but before you can stop, a strange-looking beast grabs you around the neck and throws you to the ground. You look up into a pair of bulbous, fly-like eyes set deep into a skeletal head. The figure is skinny but has the rippling muscles and scarred face of a determined, if often unsuccessful, pit fighter. You vaguely recollect hearing about a strange race of insectoids called brekkens that arrived from a distant star a few hundred years ago, but their love of the darkness and inability to work as a group has led them to become a rare and forgettable sight. Nevertheless, the one towering over you is definitely real and an immediate threat.

Sensing its attack, you roll across the concrete as a pincered arm raises sparks against it, and you leap to your feet, drawing your weapon as you do.

BREKKEN ROGUE:

Strength: 10
Health: 9

If you defeat the rogue, you may return to the street and continue looking for the Rusty Pipe. Turn to **227**.

41

You begrudgingly hand over a handful of coins, noting how soft the fur is on the creature's palm, and repeat your request. They gesture along the main road towards the monstrous flux tower that dominates the skyline. "Do you see the tower?" they say, and you turn to see where they are pointing. "Well?" you ask when they remain quiet. As you turn, you realise that they have hoodwinked you out of your money and are now a hundred yards ahead of you and disappearing quickly. You may try to pursue them (turn to **40**), or you can accept your loss by turning to **227**.

42

These steps are steeper than those leading to the first mezzanine, to the point that they are almost a step ladder. You climb them as quickly as possible until you are stood, out of breath, on the balcony. You try your hardest not to glance over the flimsy barrier that stands between you and a 40-foot dive onto the concrete below. Part of the barrier has been twisted out of shape above what looks suspiciously like a blood-stain on the distant floor. Somebody wasn't careful enough, it seems.

Heading along the balcony, you realise that somebody has propped open a window. You head towards it and see that it leads out onto another crude balcony manufactured from rusting sheets of metal and scaffolding bolted to the outer wall. Somebody seems to be sitting outside enjoying the view.

To climb through the window and talk to whoever is outside, turn to **190**. Otherwise, you may head back out into the city and begin your mission for Mandrake by turning to **196**.

43

The back-alley mechist is waiting for you in the main operating room, seemingly indifferent to the twitching body on her table. You try to avoid staring, but the creature isn't human, and whatever upgrades the surgeon is offering, you want nothing to do with it.

"Before you leave," the woman says, wiping blood from her hands, "there's something you need to know. You may have noticed that my prices are much lower than others out there. That's because the parts I use haven't all been checked to the same standards. But hey, if you wanted the best, you wouldn't be here! Right? Anyway, they are pretty stable most of the time. However, sometimes, when you go to use them, they might backfire a little bit."

She seems to notice the look of panic and anger rushing across your face. She quickly raises her hands and hurries on. "It's not a big chance, but you need to be aware of it. Just be careful."

Each time you use one of your upgrades from the back-alley mechist, you must roll a die. On a roll of 6, the upgrade fails and burns out inside you. You must deduct **4 HEALTH POINTS**, and that upgrade can no longer be used. You may not upgrade that part again. These rules only apply to upgrades carried out here at the back-alley mechist.

A betrayal like this is on another level, and you feel your rage bubbling up inside you. Revenge would be justifiable in the circumstances, but the choice remains yours. To exact revenge on the lying mechist, turn to **271**. To leave her alone and return to your search for the Rusty Pipe, turn to **236**.

44

Slowly, keeping your eyes locked on the barman's, you push the drink back towards him. Just as he looks as though he's about to explode with rage, the glass hits a sticky patch on the bar and tips, sending the vile green liquid cascading over the barman's filthy shirt. Within a second, he's over the bar and holding you up by the collar of your coat. Acting more out of instinct than thought, your hand has instinctively moved to your **PLASMA PISTOL**, and it's clear that the barman can feel the barrel pressing into his stomach.

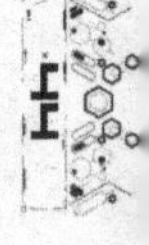

"You shoot me in here, there's a thousand people'll know what you done," he growls quietly, for your ears only.

"True," you reply with the little oxygen left in your lungs, "but you'll still be dead."

You are aware that the rest of the bar has suddenly got a lot noisier as the rest of the patrons are intensely interested in anything other than your little tussle. You're not sure who would see anything if you pulled the trigger, but on the other hand, you have a job to do in the bar. To pull the trigger anyway, turn to **47**. To put your gun away, turn to **299**.

45

A few seconds pass in silence before the eyes disappear, and the hatch slams shut. You hear a muted conversation rising swiftly to an argument before another bolt slides open, and the door swings inwards. You are greeted by a wiry man with a red face covered in blistered skin and tufts of charred hair. He is the one in possession of the broken eye upgrade and, it seems, a bad attitude. You ignore the stool that he quickly kicks away, and that was previously being used to allow him to reach the hatch in the door.

"I don't trust you," he barks, "but you know the motto, so maybe you're alright. Mandrake wouldn't send us no spies. But," and suddenly his face is filled with cruel glee, "if you turns out to be one, I'll have a lot of fun explaining why it's a bad career move. Understand?"

He doesn't wait for you to answer before shuffling you through the door and slamming it shut behind you both.

Turn to **154**.

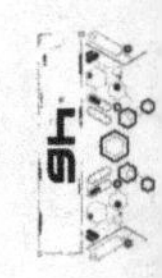

46

There is nothing of interest on the desk, only a single postcard showing a landscape on Earth that hasn't been seen for hundreds of years. You've seen these before; a sure sign that the person is deeply embedded in the Earthist cult, who believes that the Earth is still out there, waiting to be reinhabited. You shake your head and carry on looking.

Underneath the desk, you notice something lumpy hidden under an old blanket. You pull the fabric back to reveal a hatch. Opening the lid, it becomes clear that it is an escape tunnel leading away from the core. If you ever need to escape in an emergency, you would do well to turn to **82**. You make a note of that passage number and return to the mission at hand. Turn to **3**.

47

The trigger pulls back easily, and you blink in anticipation of the explosion from the barrel, but it never comes. You look up into the barman's shaking face and see a look of desperate anger. Glancing down, you see a small robot scurrying away between the legs of the crowd. You notice a glowing cube in its hands; the PlasPod for your plasma pistol. Without it, there's no charge for the plasma. Your fingers loosen on the hilt, and you hear the sound of it clattering to the floor above the rest of the noise.

You try to wrestle free of the barman's grip, but he's too strong and filled with too much rage. He drags you past the bar and into a small, dark room lit only by a flickering bare bulb hanging from the ceiling. Almost immediately, he begins to rain down with blows of his heavy fists. Only when those tire, does he move on to a thick metal bar already brown with the blood of his previous victims.

Your last thoughts as your life slips away from you are of regret. You curl into a ball, but nothing can protect you from the man's fatal blows and the world around you soon disappears into a pool of black pain.

48

You get your shot off first, but of the two fuzzy guards that you can see, you aim at the wrong one. The blast rips through the frame of the room, sending the sheet metal crashing down around you. The last thing you see before your world shrinks to a ball of cold, dark agony and then the final release of death is a rusting sheet of steel cutting towards you like a guillotine. This filthy bedroom will be where they eventually find your body - if anybody even bothers to look.

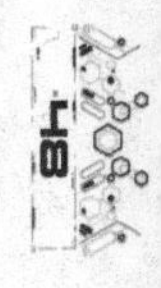

Inside the tower, the core itself glows with an eyewatering brightness. You try to watch the viscous green liquid rise through the many floors to the extraction pump high above you, but you turn away when it feels like your brain is about to leak out of your ears. It gives everything in here a harsh green highlight, washing out all other colours.

On the ground floor of the central core, there is very little to explore. An empty guard's desk sits forlornly in the middle of the space, but that is it. A set of metal steps leads up to a narrow walkway that hangs from the walls and spirals upwards to the very top of the tower. There seem to be doorways every so often along the walkway, but most of them lead to darkened rooms. About halfway up, there is a door with an illuminated window. It is too far above you to see inside, but you can see the pale yellow light battling against the overall green hue.

To check out the guards' desk, turn to **46**.

To climb the steps and head to the lighted window, turn to **3**.

The voice belongs to a twisted man hovering in the air in front of you. His face is tattooed with strange red and black lines: steel joints and metal plates cover most of his upper body. Everywhere, wires protrude from his ruptured skin. His face is lit by two glowing red eyes sitting behind a set of mirrored glasses. Inserted into his forehead are a separate set of black orbs. They blink out of time with his regular eyes. No doubt they are fitted with some form of vision-enhancing tech. You take in more of his body. Bothof his arms have been replaced with cyborg limbs powered by pistons and cogs. Chains and cables link what remains of his body to his mech limbs, while thicker wires run from his back up to the ceiling.

"We both want the same thing," he croaks as his feet touch the floor and the wires hang slack.

"Who are you?" you ask, making sure that you have a clear run to the door.

"Oh, I have many names. Most people delight in calling me the Mad Mechist." He strides towards you, grabbing you by the

chin before you can react. You try to snatch your head away, but the sharp pincers on his hand are too strong. He moves your face back and forth, looking you over like a beast at the market. Seemingly satisfied, he pushes you away and turns his back. "What scientist hasn't been called mad at some time in their career?" He lets out a hearty laugh, which quickly turns into a hacking cough. "The Mad Mechist will do for now. What's more important is how I can help you."

"You offer mech upgrades," you say. There doesn't seem to be any immediate danger, but you remain on edge.

"Amongst other things, yes. We can talk about that later. I'm more interested in helping you defeat Thundergill."

If you wish to hear what the Mad Mechist has to say, turn to **249**.

To politely refuse his offer, turn to **84**.

51

The guard's face is wracked with confusion as he tries to understand your strange request. You realise, too late, that he has nothing to do with the anarchists. His fist crashes into your face, dealing **2 HEALTH POINTS** damage and sending you bowling across the street until you come to rest against the far wall. Turn to **146**.

52

The woman approaches with a metal collar to fasten around your neck, no doubt a shock device to keep you subdued. Just as she reaches you, the cuffs snap with a satisfying sound. You roll out of her reach and spring to your feet. Your captor races to the wall and grabs a small chain-sword powered by a glowing flux cell. It hums into life, the metal spokes blurring immediately. It is only short, but one slice from that thing would be devastating. Your pack and all of your weapons have been taken from you, leaving only your fists. Your **STRENGTH** will suffer a -2 deduction during this fight.

AGENT OF THE EMPEROR:

Strength: 9
Health: 6

If you defeat the woman, turn to **135**.

53

The door opens easily, but the room
beyond it is dark. The narrow shafts of
dim light that break through a shuttered
window on the far side illuminate motes
of dust hanging in the still air. Most of
the furniture, including the broken-down
arcade machines, is scattered across the
floor, along with a desk and several chairs.
A holo-computer is still powered up in the
far corner, but you can see from where you
stand that it is locked. On the opposite wall,
a single machine seems to be clinging to
life. Soft, addictive music whistles through
the damaged speakers and the holographic
screen flickers like a detuned radio. You
approach it and recognise it as a game of
chance. As a child, you spent hours playing
similar machines without much success,
but you can attempt to correct that now. If
you'd like to play the machine, turn to **199**.
To return to the street and try the door with
the mechanical eye, turn to **97**.

54

A well-aimed hit strikes the android's central
core processor, and she slumps into a heap
on the ground. You pick over the pile to see
if there is anything worth stealing but find

nothing. You step back into the main street and continue your search for the Rusty Pipe. Turn to **28**.

55

Other than a few broken screens, a pile of rusting pipes and a battered old mattress, there is nothing in the yard bar the stack of four wooden crates. Seeing as you've fought your way here, you decide to try to break them open. You grab one of the pipes and use it to pry apart the walls of the first crate. It opens easily but is disappointingly empty. You continue with the next, the sounds of the city muffled by the towering building. The only sound is a soft scratching, probably from rats living behind the crates.

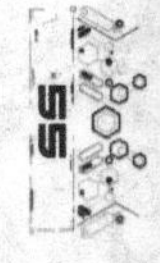

The wood of the second crate is much stronger than the first, and you quickly break into a sweat trying to prise it apart. Eventually, the nails give way, and the wooden slats clatter to the floor. You catch a glimpse of a polished steel weapon resting on the floor of the book at the same time as you hear the voice hissing and whirring behind you.

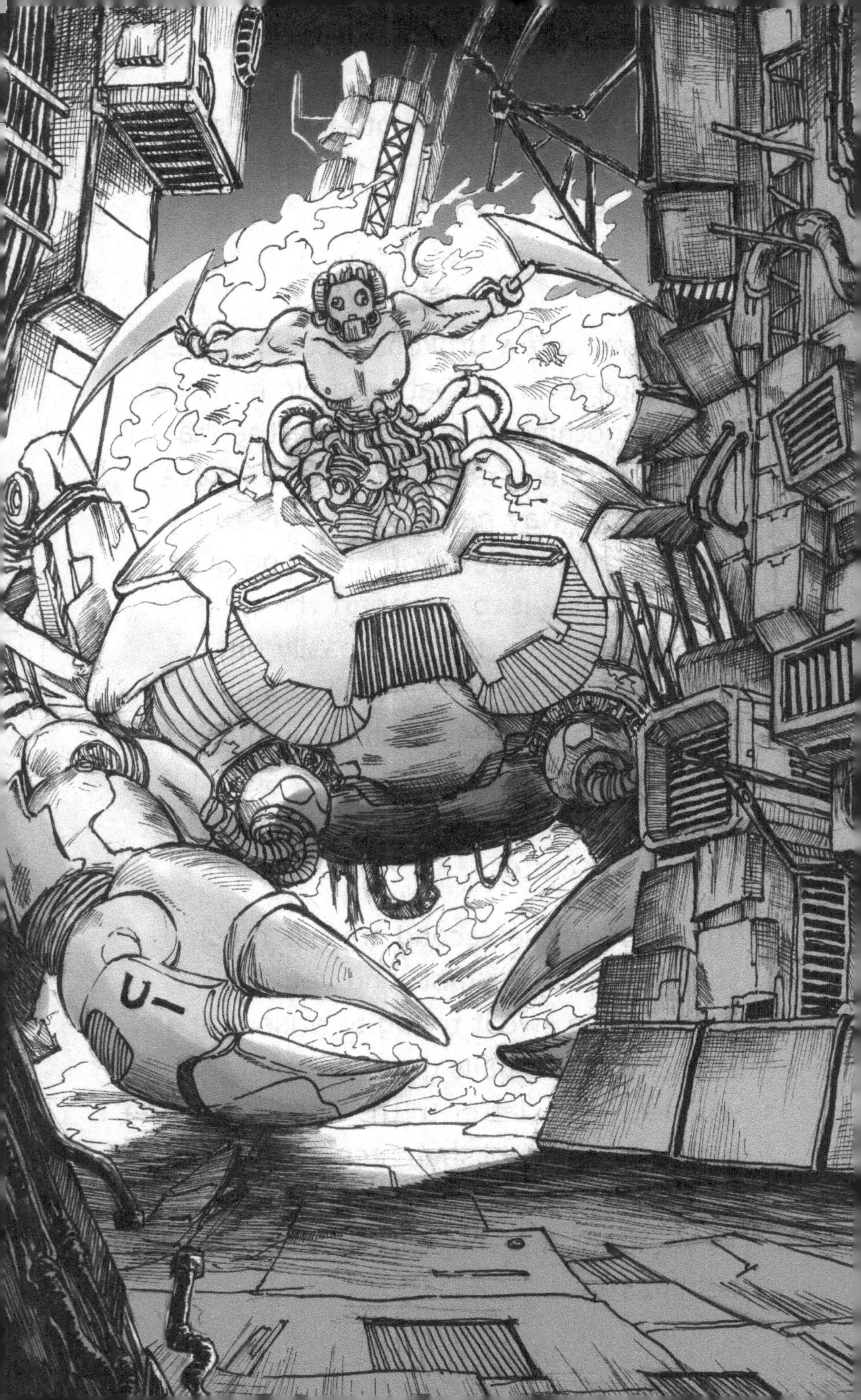

Spinning round, you realise that the scratching wasn't rats; it was the creature standing in front of you crawling down the sides of the building. You try to take it all in as it manoeuvres itself in the small space - far too small for the both of you to fight comfortably.

Mechanical, jointed legs, thin and spider-like, protrude from a skeletal shell that looks more like a crab. On top of the shell, joined by intricate cogs and thick, scorched cables, is the torso of a man. Its skin is pale, with a blue tinge, except for the thick veins that pulse with red vitality. There is no human head on the torso, only the metal visage of an android once painted yellow but now chipped and rusting. The eyes swivel in the sockets, barely able to focus on one thing at once. Each arm terminates in a sweeping blade, similar to the scythes used by ancient warriors.

Once the mechanical crab has lost half of its **HEALTH POINTS**, you may make an effort to grab the mysterious weapon from the crate. You may only do this once, and you must pass a strength test to do so. If you fail the test, the monster lands an attack whilst your back is turned, and you must reduce

your health accordingly. If you defeat the
beast, you may grab the weapon then,
regardless.

MECHANICAL CRABMAN:

Strength: 13
Health: 10

If you take the mysterious weapon at any
point, add it to your **WEAPONS**.

FAN CANON:

Strength: +4
Durability: 10
Special ability: When fired, this weapon
emits a rainbow arc of flux energy that
radiates outwards from the gun. If you are
fighting multiple enemies, roll dice against
all of them each time you fire this. If you
succeed, remove damage from each of
them. If you miss, the arc backfires and hits
you, dealing normal damage.
Keyword: **RANGED**, **ELECTRIC**

If you defeat the mechanical crabman, turn
to **121**.

56

Before the bulk of the man can crash down
and crush you beneath it, you rush from
the small enclave and head for the main
door out of the factory. You barely breath
until you are in the cooler air of the street.
You shake your head at your narrow escape
and continue your search of the dark street.
Turn to **120**.

57

The deep voice doesn't speak again until
you get close enough to smell the creature's
breath and hear its short, rasping breath.
When it does, it explains that it is running
a small store for weary travellers such as
yourself. He offers you the chance to buy
some of his wares. Make any purchases that
you desire, then turn to **301** to return to
the street.

STIM STICK (500 DING):

Each **STIM STICK** packs enough adrenaline
punch to last an entire battle. With the
powerful energy blast coursing through
your veins, you'll deal double damage
to any enemies that are unlucky enough
to stumble upon you. Not only that, any
damage you suffer will be halved.

NANOMASK (300 DING):

The nanobots contained within the mask have mild psychic powers. They use these to read the mind of any enemy you are about to face and then reform the mask into the most terrifying image for that particular mind. The shock and fear are so great that you will get an undefended attack before they come to their senses. Deal an automatic **2 HEALTH POINTS** damage to your enemy before the battle starts. This only works on the first enemy if you are fighting against a group.

TOXIC BLADE (700 DING):

This should be added to your **WEAPONS** rather than your **PACK**. The **TOXIC BLADE** is a powerful weapon that must be treated carefully. If you successfully win a round against your enemy with this weapon, then the toxic venom held within the blade is pushed into their bloodstream, quickly attacking their nervous system. In each following round of the battle, they suffer an automatic **1 HEALTH POINT** damage regardless of whether you win that round.
Strength: N/A
Durability: 1

58

Upon closer inspection, almost the entire wall of the alleyway is covered in boarded-up windows that once served as stores for a variety of exotic goods. Rusting and faded signs punctuate the brickwork here and there, but most are beyond recognition. Every so often, the door to the Rusty Pipe swings open and flood the alleyway with shredding bass and electronic hiss. You grit your teeth; *AI* music might well be the worst thing about the emperor's grip on the districts.

Several of the boards seem to be rotting through and look like they could be pried away easily enough. Three of them seem to have been hammered into place relatively recently. Each one has an old fluorescent sign hanging above it, the light long burnt out, but the letters still just about legible through the dark brown mould.

To work your way into the storefront marked as "Spike's Weapons", turn to **302**.

To look inside the storefront marked "Sweeney's Pies", turn to **255**.

To take a peek inside the room marked "Archives", turn to **200**.

59

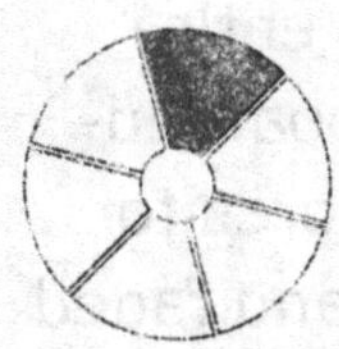

The passage bends slowly towards the east until you reach a sharp turn. You follow it round and stop. The concrete pathway continues ahead to the east, but there is also a metal hatch in the wall. It is open a crack and seems to lead to a narrow room beyond.

To enter the room, turn to **93**.

To continue east, turn to **189**.

60

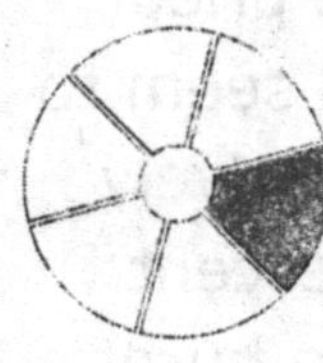

You follow the uneven pathway until you reach another junction. Ahead, the tunnel appears to split. To your right, it continues north.

To turn and head north, turn to **306**.

To continue east, turn to **259**.

61

To head to the locker, turn to **151**. To investigate the door, turn to **305**.

62

With your new information fresh in your mind, you head back out to the alleyway, where the rain drums down onto your head and creeps along your spine. A pale mist is beginning to rise from the filth-strewn brick pavement. You leave the steady beat of plasmetal music behind you and begin to look for whatever the hanging fist might be.

The alleyway seems bare, except for a few beaten-down storefronts on one side and a pile of old crates on the other. The storefronts look long-abandoned, and the crates are turning orange in the damp air.

To explore the crates, turn to **14**.

To explore the storefronts, turn to **58**.

63

The key fits the lock easily, and you swing the doors open. Inside, you find another set of doors set into the back of the locker, this time unlocked. You open those to reveal a tunnel through the back wall of the warehouse and down underground. Following it and making sure to close both sets of doors behind you, you step into the shadows. There are small, circular lamps in the wall at regular intervals, although only a handful are working. Those that are lit pulse erratically, casting enough light to see a few inches in front of you but nothing more. Arriving at the far end of the passageway, you climb another set of steps and reach an unlocked door. It leads out into yet another dark alleyway. Turn to **118**.

64

You stand awkwardly at the edge of the stall until the wisened old man looks up from a sprawling mass of wires and acknowledges you with a slight nod of his head. He taps his finger against a sign above his head, translated into the multiple different languages spoken in the slums. It simply says, ***"MECH REPAIRS"***. It seems that the man will repair any broken ***MECH UPGRADES*** for the price of 150 ***DING*** per repair. If you have any broken upgrades and wish to pay the man to fix them, you may do so now. Once you have finished your transaction, you nod your thanks and hurriedly make your way towards the steps back up into the district.

Turn to **235**.

65

"What do you want?" the barman asks in a low grumble. You order the cheapest drink you can and begrudgingly wait for him to pour a small measure of an unidentified green liquid. He slams it onto the bartop and demands 100 **DING**. If you have the money and wish to pay, turn to **177**. If you don't have the money, or you refuse to pay that amount for a drink, turn to **44**.

66

When you wake up, your head is throbbing, and your chest feels like it's on fire. You are sat, slumped against the wall, on the opposite side of the room to the door. A smell of burning hair surrounds you, and you quickly realise that the door must be electrified and you've been hit by one hell of a jolt. Remove **3 HEALTH POINTS** (or reduce your **HEALTH** to **1** if you have fewer than **4 HEALTH POINTS**). As you recover, you hear the same shrill voice crackling through the tannoy, "We told you to wait." When you feel able to move again, you stand up and await further instruction. Turn to **26**.

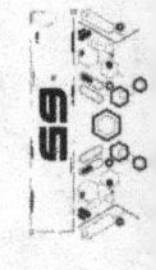

67

You pull the pin from the bomb and throw it towards the fire. It explodes in an eruption of green flux energy, wiping out half of the cultists. Roll a die and halve the total (rounding down). You must now fight that many cultists.

Turn to **195**.

68

The wall itself isn't too high and is dotted with the results of las-can battles. Each hole provides a convenient toe-hold, and you quickly reach the top, where a thin steel grating juts out over your head at a sharp angle. The metal is razor-thin and would cut through your skin if you gripped it. Besides, it's too flimsy to take your weight. You can try to twist your body to get a look over to the other side of the wall by turning to **70**. Otherwise, you must drop back down into the alleyway and enter the tower.

Turn to **87**.

69

You smash the butt of your pistol into the lock as hard as you can, but all it does is anger the **MECH WASPS**. They swarm over your hand, biting wherever they touch your skin. You stumble back, trying to shake them off, but they regroup into a thick cloud of buzzing menace. You aren't going to be able to defeat them, there are too many, and they are far too small to hit effectively. Instead, you will have to try to deflect them and then flee. Each time you win a battle round, roll a die. If you roll a 4+, you are able to break free of them and flee to the edge of the roof. If not, then you must defend another battle round until you successfully flee. You may not use any mech upgrades to flee this battle.

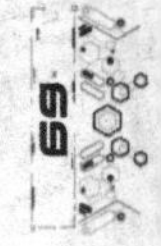

MECH WASPS:

Strength: 6
Health: N/A

If you successfully flee to the edge of the roof, you are able to scramble back onto the platform and ride it down to the street below. The nanobots remain on the roof. Turn to **236**.

You pull the sleeves of your coat down far enough to wrap around your hands and reach out to get a better grip. The metal digs into the leather but doesn't quite reach your skin. Twisting and folding yourself, you slip between the grating and pull yourself up onto the lip of concrete at the top of the wall. At the last second, your hand slips, and you slump forward into the nest of barbed wire. It slices into your face and lacerates the palm of your hand where your coat has slipped. Deduct **2 HEALTH POINTS** and reduce your **STRENGTH** by 1 due to your injured hand.

It takes a few seconds for your breathing to return to normal and to recover your balance, but you have a reasonable view of the other side of the wall. It seems that there is nothing beyond it except for a small, square yard, maybe eight feet wide on each side. There is a stack of wooden crates piled up just below you, but that's it.

To try to pull yourself over the wall and onto the crates, turn to **186**.

If you have finished exploring, you may carefully drop back into the alleyway and enter the tower. Turn to **87**.

Upon your approach, the woman startles and coughs hard into a filthy handkerchief. After she has calmed down, cursing your disturbance as she does, she stands and waddles to the back of the van, where she introduces herself as a pharmacist. She doesn't seem interested in hiding the fact that her medicines are unlabelled and most-likely stolen, but she also doesn't seem too inclined to offer you any kind of deal if you choose to buy any.

VORTEX SYRUP (100 DING):

A sickly syrup made from whatever chemicals the woman had to hand, the **VORTEX SYRUP** comes in plated test-tubes. The liquid swirls and dances inside without any outside interference. She promises you that each vial will restore **4 HEALTH POINTS**.

MIND SHIELD (350 DING):

Each **MIND SHIELD** tablet is the size of a small lozenge and has a strange, bioluminescent quality. In the darkness of the alleyway, it glows eerily. When taken before a confrontation, the **MIND SHIELD** will prevent any enemy from being able to read or control your mind. Perfect for meetings with espers.

RED RAGE (200 DING):

Mixed with the adrenaline of a pit fighter and a space orc's sweat, **RED RAGE** is a stimulant that will destroy any inhibitions you have during a fight. Fighters from the long-lost civilisation of Tyrinth used to imbibe before battle to give them an extra edge. Drinking the vile liquid will increase your **STRENGTH** by 3 for the length of one battle.

Once you have decided on any purchases, remove the **DING** from your **PACK** and return to the street. Turn to **256**.

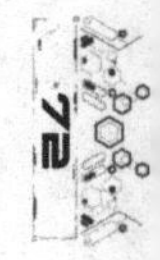

72

You brush the area of skin that the surgeon told you would activate your gauntlet, and sure enough, there is a small ridge under the skin. You push it quickly and feel your hand strengthen almost immediately. If this is a back-alley upgrade, make the usual test to see if it malfunctions. If it does, turn to **170**. If you manage to activate it successfully, you use it to rip the slime from your arm and toss it to the floor. It hisses and tries desperately to form a shape before settling into the rough outline of a snarling black dog. Turn to **122**.

73

You land in a stinking pile of filth, your arms disappearing up to your elbows. Mercifully, you manage to keep your face clear of the sludge and slowly wiggle until you are free to move again. You scramble over the pile and slide down the other side, moving forward until you reach a shadowy area filled with hushed whispers.

Turn to **321**.

74

"I see you took my gift," Mandrake says, pointing to the card that hangs from your waist. "Nobody should bother you in here while you wear it. On the other hand, it comes with a price. So does that new heart of yours. You owe me."

"I was coming here to help you anyway,"

you say, accepting her invitation to sit in a comfortable, if battered, leather recliner opposite the desk.

"Yes," she says and grins widely and mercilessly, "but you were hoping to get paid. I suggest that you're already in my debt. Do what you came here to do, and we'll call it square."

You erupt at the audacity of her expecting you to work for free, but the pain in your chest forces you to sit back down, breathless and on the verge of tears.

If you're still interested in hearing what Mandrake has to say, turn to **202**.

Otherwise, turn to **115**.

75

The stairs lead quickly to a tram station platform. Most of the punters are arriving from a much larger set of stairs to one side; you appear to have entered via a service stairwell. Nonetheless, a single tram carriage swiftly pulls in, and the doors open. You race inside and glance at the chipped and scratched buttons that indicate each destination. The one for **CENTRAL UPPER** is dimmed out, but the other three are glowing.

Choose your destination:

EAST STATION (Turn to **160**)

WEST STATION (Turn to **270**)

CENTRAL LOWER STATION (Turn to **164**)

76

Just as you begin to consider where to head next, you hear Mandrake's voice shouting down from the mezzanine above. She knows you're hear and wants to speak to you. She doesn't seem angry, but there is an urgency to her voice. You take the hint and head to the stairs up to the next floor. Turn to **109**.

77

The alleyway continues for a few hundred metres before turning off to the left. On the corner, an old woman is slumped in a chair by the side of a rusted and broken-down truck. The rear doors are hanging open, but you can't see what is inside from where you are. To approach the woman and investigate the van, turn to **71**. To ignore it and follow the passage to the left, turn to **256**.

78

You arrive at a crossroads. In one direction is the towering fence that surrounds the flux tower and the factory that it supports. In another, the road disappears into darkness, with very few people heading in that direction. The final road seems to lead past another tram station. There seems to be a broken-down warehouse some way in the distance, past a pulsing glow emanating from a shadowy alley.

To head towards the flux tower, turn to **131**.

To head along the dark road, turn to **290**.

To head towards the pulsing light and broken-down factory, turn to **98**.

79

You pick over the bodies of the guards and take an ***ELECTROBLADE***. The handle is stout but light, and the blade itself hums quietly with the electrical energy that courses through it. You've seen them before and

know that the flux batteries don't last for long before they need to be replaced. It'll definitely be fun to use while it lasts, so you add it to your **WEAPONS** and head through the gate into the district. Once you are inside, you stop and take in your surroundings. Turn to **234**.

ELECTROBLADE:

Strength: +6
Durability: 2
Keyword: **ELECTRIC**

80

"Stim sticks?" you ask over the ear-splitting noise. The stallholder shrugs and points to a sign painted on the front of one of the barrels. It has been translated into every language spoken in the diverse melting pot of the slums but simply tells you that the packs are called **RES-STICKS**. You try your best to imply to the old woman behind the stall that you don't understand, and she seems to get the message.

Rolling her shoulders back almost as much as her eyes, she performs a simple mime of somebody being killed. She then takes a pack and presses it against her chest, at which point she mimes being resurrected and, by the looks of things, full of energy.

It becomes clear that **RES-STICKS** are resurrection sticks, capable of bringing a recently deceased body back to life, if only for a few short moments. They can be invaluable in a skirmish and can be used to allow one of your allies to continue fighting after they have been killed. They will only survive until the end of the battle, after which point the adrenaline will wear off, and they will succumb to their fate, but that might be enough to be the difference between life and death for you.

Each **RES-STICK** costs 500 **DING**. You buy any that you need, add them to your **PACK**, and make your way hastily towards the steps back to the surface.

Turn to **235**.

81

"There is another way," says a deep voice from the side of the room. "There's a tunnel that leads underneath the outer gates. It's dangerous, and I don't know how you'll get into the core when you get there." A tall man, covered in thick grey fur, steps out of the shadows.

"This is Killik," Mandrake says, introducing you to the man. "He's our head of investigative exploration."

"A spy," he says, extending his hand with a smile. You shake it, and he continues explaining his plan. "If you leave this building and take the first turn, you'll come to a metal door in a sturdy metal wall. Ignore that. Instead, look for a manhole cover buried underneath some rubbish. It's not locked, you just need to give it a bit of a whack sometimes to get it to open. That will lead you to a system of tunnels, which will take you underneath the gate. The air is toxic down there," he adds. "Stick to the wooden walkway, and you'll be fine. If you get lost, try to find it as quickly as possible and try to head north."

"And when we get to the core?" you ask.

"It'll be guarded. The workers will all have cards to get past it. You might have to be a bit more forceful unless you can find

another way in once you get there. None
of us have ever been beyond the gate, so
we've no idea what you'll find there."

"Good luck," Mandrake offers as you open
the door and step back out into the night.
"We are counting on you."

You head back along the street until you
reach the turning. Turn to **287**.

82

You drop down into the escape tunnel
beneath the guards' desk. Strong lights
hang from the ceiling, but the tunnel itself
winds slowly away, so you can't see any
further forwards than a few dozen yards.
You set off at a spring, ignoring your
burning lungs and aching legs. After a
minute or so, you begin to hear the ragged
breathing of somebody up ahead. You
redouble your efforts and quickly emerge
into a large hanger.

A large haulage ship occupies most of the
hanger landing pad. It's burners are at
full capacity, and the cargo door is slowly
lowering. You race forward as quickly as
possible but realise with a sinking horror
that Thundergill is going to reach the

platform in time. Sure enough, as it crashes to the concrete, he is only a hundred yards away from it.

Stopping suddenly, you drop to your knees and draw your weapon. You've got one chance to pull off the shot of a lifetime and take him down. You will need to test your strength. For this test, you may choose any weapon in your possession and use its **STRENGTH** modifier to help with your test.

If you pass the test, turn to **142**.

If you fail, turn to **37**.

83

Slowly, you feel the sense of numbness withdraw from your body, and your eyes begin to open and adjust to the flickering fluorescent light hanging over you. You wait until you are sure your legs can take your weight before spinning slowly onto your feet and gathering your belongings.

If this is your first visit to the mechist, turn to **43**. Otherwise, return to the section you were at before you visited this septic surgery. Remember the instructions the surgeon gave you after your first operation.

84

The mechist hisses and spins on his heels to face you. "You fool," he growls. For a moment, he seems ready to attack, but he manages to control his temper and fix his face in a grimace. "Should you change your mind," he offers through gritted teeth, "I shall be here waiting."

You thank him for the offer and leave through the red door. Behind you, you hear him raging in the darkness of his home, but you don't turn back. You push on to the junction, where you continue straight and follow the road around the corner. Turn to **268**.

85

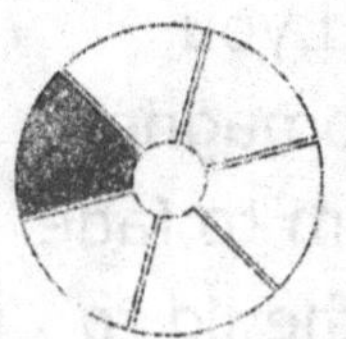

You follow the wooden walkway along the narrow sewers, ducking as the ceiling lowers. Before long, you are forced to your knees and continue on all fours until you reach a bend. The ceiling rises again, and the walkway veers eastwards. You push on until you reach another junction. The wooden walkway bends suddenly and heads north. To the east and the south, there is a concrete causeway that appears to run for a long way in both directions. The southern passageway is particularly dark, and you are sure that you can hear the sound of something moving around. A small trickle of toxic waste runs along a central channel, but there is no other sign of sewage.

To head east, turn to **60**.

To head south, turn to **243**.

To head north, turn to **23**.

86

You take **THUNDERGILL'S PROSTHETIC EYE** from your **PACK** and hold it up to the retina scanner. A purple beam races across the bloodshot sphere, and the lock beeps. Somewhere inside, gears turn, and you hear the familiar hum of an electromagnet powering down. The nanobots seem to fade away to nothing, like a mist, and the lid to the crate pops open a fraction. Turn to **176**.

87

The interior of the tower is dimly lit by flickering neon tubes pinned to the walls at odd intervals. Over the years, each one

...s been replaced with whatever tubes the
anarchists could find, and the end result is a
kaleidoscopic assault of headache-inducing
light. You try your best to block it out and
move in the hideout.

In the dim light, it's hard to get an accurate
handle on the size of the space, but you
guess that it's roughly a hundred feet in
each direction. It's mainly open, with a few
small rooms clumsily built out from the
walls using wood, sheet metal and whatever
else was to hand. They seem to provide the
only privacy on this floor.

Just ahead of you, you can see a guard
slumped in a chair. A couple of empty
bottles are scattered around his feet, and
he doesn't seem inclined to wake up at
your entrance. Looking at his pallid skin,
you aren't completely sure he isn't already
dead.

Beyond the guard, there is a circular glass
column that glows faintly with a green glow.
It's narrower than the professional systems
inside the core, but you instantly recognise
it as a flux mining pump. No doubt it's an
illegal operation that the anarchists are
running.

There appear to be three main rooms in the space and a set of stairs leading up to a grated mezzanine floor that runs around the inside edge of the tower. To your right, there is a long room made of damp and moulding wood. Ahead of you, on the far side of the room, is another wide room constructed from sheet metal. The third room has been crudely built in the space underneath the stairs.

If you'd like to look more closely at the guard, turn to **260**.

Otherwise, turn to **31**.

88

Mandrake's plan to destroy Thundergill is simple enough. You and any **ALLIES** you have will try to sneak into the factory. There, you will make your way into the central tower and try to seek him out. "He'll be hiding away in his apartment at the top of the core," Mandrake explains. "He never leaves it, and he'll be unguarded if you can get in."

"How will we get into the core?" you ask.

"It's not going to be easy," Mandrake says. "Getting past the gates will be hard enough. Only union factory workers have access."

If you have **UNION CARDS** in your **PACK**, turn to **100**.

If not, turn to **81**.

89

You make your way back towards the steps as quickly as possible, making your best effort not to draw attention to yourself. Just as you reach the bottom and begin your climb up into the foetid air of the district, you hear a shout behind you. Whoever it is has identified you, and they don't seem friendly. You ignore the noises that follow and slip out into the night, shaking free your assailer before they even come close to catching you. You retrace your steps back towards the side street and continue along your way. Turn to **231**.

90

You race back along the dark streets until you reach the junction. Turning left, you head back to the main road. The flux core is glowing brighter than ever, casting its own green shadow over everything. You turn and look for the steps up to the tram station. Turn to **128**.

91

The man is far enough away that the trek to his dwelling seems ominous. You are sure that you feel the prying eyes of strangers piercing your back with every step. The towering monolith of the industrial factory peers down at you, the air belching from the spires at the top its own acrid breath. Exposed wires and dangling cables form a spider's web of washing lines across the shanty town, forcing you to duck every so often and take your eyes off the man. Every step feels like a trap, the expectation that he will be upon you growing with each second, but he remains in his doorway, silhouetted against a small fire burning in a barrel behind him.

When you finally reach him, he steps out of the way and beckons you inside. You accept his offer, taking a seat on a damp roll of old carpet wedged against the tin walls. The distant hum of machinery, the heartbeat of the factory's ceaseless operations, seems far away.

"You don't belong here," the man says again. "You are too alive to belong inside these walls."

"What do you want?" you ask, reaching slowly for your weapon.

"You won't need that, don't worry," he says, laughing. He turns his back and flicks the switch on an old kettle, a relic of a bygone age. "Grime?" he asks, flicking a spoonful of the popular, if rancid, drinking powder into a filthy mug. You shake your head.

"Never been a fan," you say. "I prefer coffee."

"Hah! You need to be on the fifth level or higher to get that nowadays. Just grime down here. Grime and despair."

"Why did you call me over?"

The man takes a sit, moving his face into the flickering light of the fire. Now that you look at him closely, he's much younger than you and healthy compared to the other residents of the district. "You want to get rid

of Thundergill." It was a simple statement with no questions attached. "I can help."

"How do you know-" you begin before being interrupted.

"We all do," he says patiently. "Nobody comes past the gate who don't belong here unless they are after Thundergill. It don't matter how you got in here," he continues, sipping noisily on the thick brown sludge, "you won't get no further. The scum that guards the central core are fully 'droid, there's no human there. They can't be tricked, and they won't move. Unless you've got a verified union card, which I doubt you have, you're stuck."

"If I've not got one of those, how do I get past?" you ask, growing tired of the man's riddles.

"You attack them with a disrupter grenade. It's like a flashbang but for 'droids. It buggers their circuits for a minute, or too, then you can just run past them."

"What about cameras?"

"The 'droids are the cameras. If they're out,

they ain't seeing anything. O' course, when they come back online, every alarm in the place will go off, and you'll need to be inside the core or running like hell by then. You should be fine once you are inside the core, though."

"Won't Thundergill go into hiding when he hears the alarm?"

"He's already in hiding. The only way he could be more locked up is if they sent him to **Hunzen VI.**"

"The prison planet," you mutter.

"Exactly. He ain't getting no more secure no matter what happens. That's why I don't mind telling you how to get in. It ain't gonna make a jot of difference."

"Don't you want him gone?" You are astounded that anybody could support a cruel master like Thundergill.

"I want to get paid. While he's there, I'm getting paid. If he's gone, who knows what will happen."

You thank the man for his time and get up to leave. "Take this," he says to your back as you duck under the door frame. He throws you a small metal canister. "A disrupter grenade." You add **DISRUPTER GRENADE** to your **PACK**.

"Thanks," you say again and step out into the night.

Turn to **224**.

92

Sparks fly from the cables holding the mechist upright. Several of them leap onto the bookshelves, igniting the dry paper like kindling. Within seconds, the room is ablaze, removing any chance you had to explore further. You leave the mechist wheezing in a heap on the floor and push through the door back out into the street. You slam it shut and try to block out the screams from inside. The heat against the metal is already terrifying. The metal walls of the building should stop it from spreading into the rest of the street, but you make yourself scarce just in case. You sprint through the dark street and head straight on at the junction. Turn to **268**.

93

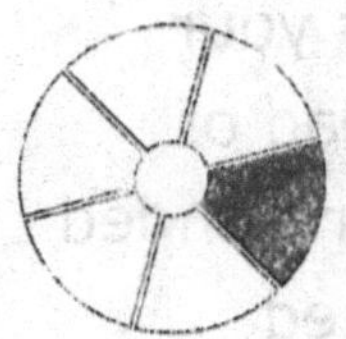

You climb through the hatch and drop down into a dark room. On first inspection, it seems to be empty, but your arrival has disturbed a colony of large bats high above you. You duck as the first one swoops down and try to swing the hatch open for them to escape. Instead, they seem intent on attacking you. Their demonic red eyes penetrate the darkness just as they intend to use their teeth and claws to penetrate your skin.

Roll a die. The number indicates how many bats you must destroy before you are able to flee.

BAT:
Strength: 6
Health: 5

Once you manage to break free, you scramble back through the hatch and slam it shut behind you. You continue along the tunnel to the east. Turn to **189**.

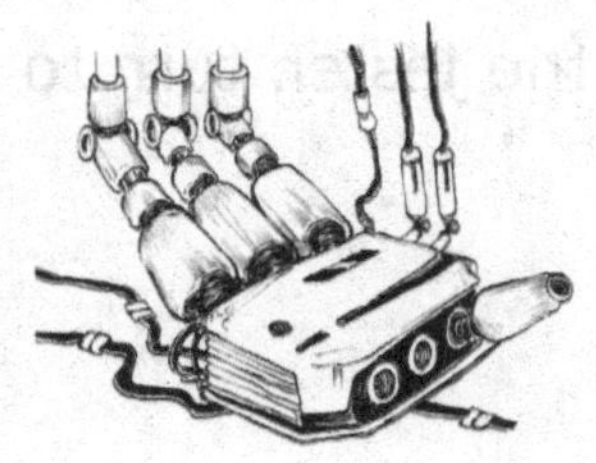

The sound of low laughter reaches your ears before you see what's up ahead of you. Within an instant, you are surrounded by slender figures, each one dressed in chequered patterns of bright pink, turquoise and purple. Each one is wearing a featureless black mask over their face. You recognise them at once as Jongleurs, one of the more deadly clans from your youth.

There are three of them surrounding you, but you know that their resolve has always been weak. If you can defeat one of them, the others will likely flee. For every round of the battle, you must roll a die. On a roll of 6, your attention is drawn by their juggling, and they hit you with a lightning-quick attack. You must remove *1 HEALTH POINT* each time this happens.

JONGLEUR:

Strength: 9
Health: 10

If you defeat the jester, turn to **309**.

Sweeney's Pies!
revolution
RISE
WITH PIES

You turn the corner and stop dead in your tracks. Acting on impulse, you duck behind the wreck of a burnt-out tank. The road here is long, perhaps a few hundred feet, and bordered by the backs of buildings. There are no doors or windows here. It is nothing more than a forgotten space between habs. Ahead, maybe halfway along the road, a group of people are gathered around a burning metal drum.

It is unclear how old the people are or whether they are all humanoid, but they are all wearing the same outfit. Each one is dressed in a long grey hooded sweatshirt, with heavy service-issue trousers and steel-capped boots. They look almost military, but the Emperor's army is nothing more than a distant memory in these parts. On their backs, they are wearing bright red backpacks, which connect to each one's gas mask through a thick hose. When you catch a glimpse of their faces, they are hidden behind the bulging smoked glass of their mask. Each one is armed with a long metal baton, their fingers capped with knuckle dusters.

The cultists themselves aren't the strangest thing in the street. Rising out of the burning bin is the flickering image of a man made entirely of metal. Where the body is broken, flames lick and splutter, giving him the appearance of firey blood. He doesn't seem fully-formed, but the cultists that surround him are chanting themselves into a frenzy, screaming the same unintelligible words over and over. With each repetition, the visage seems to grow more solid. You can't work out if the metal man is moving as he grows or if the heat of the fire is casting an optical illusion.

Whatever is happening, you decide to put a stop to it. If you have a **FLUX GRENADE** in your **PACK**, you may choose to use it now by turning to **67**. If you don't have one or are choosing not to use one, turn to **144**.

96

The outer wall hasn't been maintained here, and you notice several patches of dark rust and other signs that the citizens of the slum have tried to force their way in. Two guards, dressed in the golden armour and clan gear of the Imperialists, are stood to attention on either side of the narrow gate. You can sense the power of the Emperor flowing through them. His unofficial guards look every bit as powerful as he is.

The gate is open, but you are unsure whether you can sprint through before they attack. You feel the weight of your pistol in your pocket and consider your options.

Other than trying to casually walk past the guards, you may try to sneak past to find a way through the rusting wall, or you can draw your gun and attempt to pick them off from a distance. You realise your chances of this succeeding are slim.

To walk up to the guards and try to enter the district, turn to **261**.

To attempt to sneak past to find another way in, turn to **191**.

To try to pick them off with your weapon, turn to **276**.

97

The mechanical eye turns in its socket and follows your movements as you approach the door. It doesn't seem to trigger an alarm, so you open the door and proceed through to the other side. Turn to **239**.

98

You follow the narrow road until you reach the source of the pulsing light. Standing eight-feet tall and built from solid metal, you are standing in the flux-green glow of what must be the MindPod that you have been sent to destroy. Turn to **34**.

99

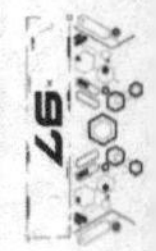

The rusted hinges give way easily, and the door crashes to the concrete floor. You recoil at the echoing sound, but you don't appear to have drawn any immediate attention. Entering the building, you find yourself in a vast and airy warehouse. Unlike most of the district, this space seems to have been kept fairly clean. Flickering orange lights illuminate the space, albeit with strange, animated shadows. The floor, ceiling and walls have been painted a clinical white, although dark grease spots are scattered throughout the building. Overhead, an intricate system of chains runs from one side to the other and front to back. Hanging from the chains are thousands of androids in various states of completion. Some are indistinguishable from those walking around in the streets, whereas others are nothing more than a torso overflowing with twisted wires and blinking sensors. You've head these places be referred to as "meat" warehouses in the past, and there is definitely a grim similarity between the production lines in front of you and the deconstruction lines in the abattoirs outside the district walls.

You push further into the space, trying not to knock against the hanging bodies where you can. The whole room feels dead and lifeless, but there is something about the lifeless shells of the androids that feels almost like a paused breath, as though they will stir to life at any point. Shaking that hideous thought from your mind, you make your way to the far side of the room, where you discover a desk strewn with half-completed projects. One of them appears

G-3

to be a visor. It is attached to a helmet, although the connections don't seem to be the most secure. If you wish to try the helmet on, turn to **173**. Otherwise, turn to **125**.

100

One of Mandrake's crew shoots forward and grabs the cards from your hand. "These are real," he says, taking a close look at one and scanning it with his watch. "All filled with dummy information. They'll get you past the gate, at least."

"Can they get them into the core?" Mandrake asks urgently.

"Not like this. I'll need to change the codes to make them appear to be verified. It'll take me a few minutes, but I can do it."

Whilst the tech guy races off to do what he needs to, Mandrake explains the final parts of the new plan. Getting through the gates should be easy now, she explains, but you must avoid drawing any attention to yourself. The Imperial guards are on the lookout for any rebels, so it's important to present yourself as a broken-down worker and nothing more.

When the man returns with enough cards for you all, Mandrake gives you all a hug and guides you towards the door. "Head to the main gate," she tells you, "and good luck."

With that, you are gently pushed through the door, which slams shut behind you.

Update the **UNION CARDS** in your **PACK** to be **VERIFIED UNION CARDS** and turn to **104**.

101

"You're no better than her," Pygon screams at you, storming back through the window.

She slams it shut behind her, and you hear the sickening sound of a bolt being slid into place. Your only way back in is to smash the window using the chair that she left behind. Test your strength. If you are successful, the chair smashes through the glass, and you escape without harm. If not, then the shattering glass slices into your arm, and you suffer **2 HEALTH POINTS** damage. Either way, you manage to climb back through onto the balcony. Pygon is long gone, so you scramble back down the steps and head out into the city. Turn to **196**.

102

The gall of the creature riles you, and you huff at their suggestion. You barge past them and out into the middle of the road. You determine to find the place yourself and follow the main road further into the district. Turn to **227**.

103

The surgeon swipes the screen, and a list of available upgrades flashes into focus. Each one is accompanied by a price: cheap compared to one of the licensed mechists in the heart of the district.

NIGHT VISION
120 DING (turn to 229)

SKELETAL STRENGTHENING
300 DING (Turn to 322)

PISTON LEGS
200 DING (Turn to 206)

POWER GAUNTLET
200 DING (Turn to 188)

SILVER-TONGUED MICROCHIP
400 DING (Turn to 158)

To purchase any of these items, turn to the number in brackets next to the item. Remember to mark this section. You may return here to add more upgrades whenever you are within the city, and you are not engaged in a battle. If you do, make a note of the section you are leaving before heading here, you will need it in order to return to your adventure.

If you would sooner not upgrade at this time, you may leave with the surgeon's blessing. If this is the first time you have visited the room, you may return to the street by turning to **266**. Otherwise, return to your previous section.

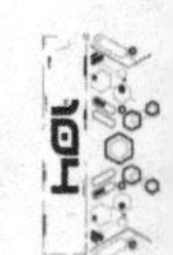

104

Your journey back to the main gateway to the factory is uneventful, and you soon arrive at the checkpoint. A queue of broken and silent bodies slowly makes its way forward. You note how they scan their **ID** card before being allowed through a lasergate. The gate only stays open for a few seconds before snapping shut, regardless of whether the unfortunate worker has made it through. You wince as one worker, an alien from a distant system with a body that shows signs of severe torture, stumbles as they step through the open gateway. With a sickening sound of meat being sliced, the lasergate snaps shut, sending parts of the poor creature's body tumbling in different directions. Even before it has stopped rolling, a pair of meat-hoarders scurry out of the shadows and drag the body away. Rumours of these harvesters have abounded for decades, but you've never really believed them. The idea of the dead meat of the slums being recycled into food for the lowest and hungriest is repellant, and yet this close to the core, people cling to life in whatever ways they can.

Eventually, you step up to the gate. Your heart is racing, beating out a deafening drumbeat against your ribs as you place your forged **ID** card against the scanner. A sense of relief washes over you when the machine blinks and beeps and the lasergate flashes open. You rush through, along with any **ALLIES**, and step into the desolate wasteland that surrounds the main factory core. Even this close to the flux lines, people have set up home. Buildings have sprouted like toadstools, made from whatever scrap material is lying around. Narrow streets weave their way between small huts and lean-tos. Some have even built precarious sheds that cling to the outer fences like bird's nests. The rusting beams used to support them barely seem strong enough, and yet they hold.

Even this late at night, a steady throng of people is moving through the slum. It gives the impression of an entirely separate town, part of District U and yet not. Nobody seems to have noticed your arrival, or perhaps you fit into this wretched nest of despair more than you would like to admit.

To ignore the slums and head straight for the central tower, turn to **224**.

To explore the slums, turn to **116**.

105

As you approach the window, you stop and duck back into the corner. A pair of muscled hands grip the windowsill, and you hear the grunt of a heavy-set man pulling himself into the room. You cower into the shadows, hoping that he doesn't see you, but his mech-eyes swivel in his skull until you see the soft green tint of night vision. You're busted, and suddenly he looks even bigger in the cramped space of the room. His muscles ripple with the effects of flux injections, and thick wires run the lengths of his arms and legs, connecting them to the power system installed somewhere within his massive frame. For somebody living in the damp shell of an old weapons store, the man is sporting some serious upgrades.

CYBORG SQUATTER:

Strength: 14

Health: 6

If you overcome him, you flee to the alleyway in case some form of technomancy wakes him from the dead, and you have to kill him all over again. Turn to **133**.

106

The door to the room under the stairs is locked with a heavy padlock. There is a three-digit rolling lock that can be used to unlock it. If you know the code, turn to that number now. If not, turn to **76**.

With every passing second, Thundergill gets further away. After a few minutes, you realise that it is too late. He's gone. By the time you find him, he will be entrenched in another hideout, well-guarded and impenetrable. You have failed, both at exacting your revenge and saving District-U from his tyranny. Even holed up in a distant bunker, his power will reach far enough to pull the strings here. You collapse to your knees and sob.

After a few moments, you feel a hand grip your shoulder and glance up into the furious eyes of Mandrake. "You failed," she hisses. "There is no place for failure here. I need anarchists who do whatever it takes to get the job done. You're no longer welcome in District-U, do you understand? I'll make sure that every clan leader knows who you are. Even the virulents won't accept you. Get off this planet and never come back."

She doesn't wait for your reply, although you don't know what to say anyway. You know in your heart that she's not wrong. You had him in your sights, and you failed.

What little life you have left will have to be spent elsewhere. This isn't the ending you had in mind when you stepped through the district gates, but it's the ending you've written. Bad luck.

108

In defence against the heat, most of the windows have been propped open, and many have heads thrust through them, trying to sell whatever they have available. Some are offering food, others drugs. Yet others are offering black-market cybernetic mods, guaranteed to make you see the light. You shuffle past until you find one at ground level that seems at least marginally clean. A beautiful young woman with skin the colour of the ocean and dark orange hair to her shoulders leans out and reads you the menu. Everything has a cost in the slums, and the weight of the ding in your wallet must take a hit if there's anything you wish to buy.

NOURISHING GRUEL (200 DING): Made with Sanctorian oats and sand worm livers, this gruel will restore your health to maximum.

FLUX GRENADE (300 DING):

Outlawed across the Wide, flux grenades are devasting weapons that can destroy an entire clan in one go. When deployed, it will inflict **8 HEALTH POINTS** damage to your enemy. That damage comes at a cost, though. Nobody can escape the power of the grenade. When you use it, you must roll a die. You suffer that many **HEALTH POINTS** damage yourself. Use wisely.

GRIT BISCUIT (50 DING):

These tasteless snacks are made from the grit in the street, along with several rare herbs. They aren't pleasant to eat, but each one will restore **3 HEALTH POINTS**.

Make your purchases and turn to **96**.

109

The metal steps echo under your heavy boots, but the guard barely stirs. Nevertheless, you proceed as quietly as possible and soon emerge onto the metal walkway that clings to the walls of the tower. Overhead, there seems to be another mezzanine, but it only clings to one wall. You follow the walkway round, past a locked door, until you reach the far wall of the building. There, another room seems to have been built onto the outside wall of the tower. Access is through a hole cut into the concrete wall itself. If you'd like to look inside, turn to **319**. If you'd sooner continue along the passageway, turn to **264**.

110

The large roller door is locked and heavily bolted, but a smaller door to one side seems weak enough to break through. Test your strength. If you are successful, turn to **99**. If not, you return to the street and continue your journey. Turn to **120**.

111

You join the queue of silent bodies moving steadily towards the entrance gate. Nobody says a word, and you are grateful for the time to think quickly about your next move. If your card doesn't scan, will there be an alarm? You quickly scout the area for a swift escape if needed. The street is far too open to hide. Your only route out of here seems to be to head back to the main road and try to blend into the crowd, but who knows if

that will be enough. By the time you finally reach the gate, you are sweating into your thick jacket, although your own smell goes someway to masking the foul odour of the bodies around you.

With a profound sense of relief, your card scans successfully, and the gate snaps open. You race through, eager to avoid the meat-hoarders, and it slides shut behind you. Most of the crowd is heading for their shift inside the central tower. To follow them, turn to **224**. Even inside the walls of the factory, slum buildings have sprouted like toadstools. There seems to be a small but steady throng of people moving amongst them, trading items and sharing secrets. To break from the line of workers and explore the inner-slums, turn to **116**.

112

The guard swims in and out of focus, at times multiplying into two or three versions of himself. You pick your favourite, aim, and squeeze the trigger. You blink with the force of the recoil, something that's never even registered before, and hear the satisfying thud of the guard crashing into the metal wall. Taking the opportunity, you stab the needle into your arm and cry out as hot lead rushes through your veins and squeezes your brain in a vice. It passes in seconds, leaving behind only a shadow and a scar in your memory. You'll need to get your chest stitched up, but it's given you the energy to stand, at least, and your vision seems to be returning to normal. However, you are still incredibly weak and barely clinging to life. Reduce your **HEALTH** to 1 **POINT**. You may not use any items in your **PACK** to restore any more health until you are told otherwise. Turn to **180**.

113

"There no answers here," he mutters in the same broken language as before. "Only me." Before you can react, he lashes out with his fist, cracking you squarely in the stomach. You collapse into a heap, the wind forced from your body, and scramble away to the far side of the street. Turn to **146**.

114

Sure enough, you hear the sound of movement somewhere outside the door as soon as you stand up. You hasten over to the wall and try to pry one of the bricks out of the wall. You manage to claw it free just as a wretched excuse of a man bursts through the door. He is shorter than average, although that is made worse by his twisted and hunched-back. He is bent double until his chin almost rests on the filthy floor, his wide eyes staring up at you from his shrivelled head. His jaw has been broken badly in the past and hangs open at a strange angle, whereas both of his ears are missing. Scars map out a terrible game of misfortune across his face, and the pungent smell of decay hits you almost immediately.

You take in all of this information in a split second, but the guard is quicker than he looks. In that moment, he is upon you, trying to snatch the brick from your grasp. Test your strength. If you are successful, turn to **310**. Otherwise, turn to **211**.

115

You wince at the searing pain in your chest but manage to stand. "Forget it," you curse and stumble towards the door.

"If you leave now, Thundergill will win," Mandrake says flatly. "We need all the help we can get. I think the trade for your new heart is more than fair. Leave if you like, but you know too much for me to let you live."

To leave anyway, turn to **240**. If you'd sooner reluctantly accept her offer, turn to **202**.

116

This close to the factory core, the slums nestle together even closer than on the outside. People are living almost on top of each other, with the simple dirty beds being used by whoever needs to sleep. Filth and disease are rife. You try not to step too close to those whose skin is sloughing or who are covered with pustules. After a few twists and turns through the maze-like tracks between the shacks, your exploration seems to be a poor choice. Just as you turn to try to navigate your way back to the core, somebody shouts out to you from one of the open doorways.

"You don't belong here," he says. His voice doesn't sound angry or accusatory, more matter-of-fact.

You glance around, but nobody else is paying any attention to either of you, and he is clearly addressing you. You can head over to him to tell him to keep it quiet, or you can ignore him and try to find your way back.

To talk to the man, turn to **91**.

To head back and follow the line of workers towards the core, turn to **224**.

117

You are greeted by a wall of noise. The music is at an eye-watering level, and the general sound of arguments fills in the gaps. The air is filled with thick, sour-smelling smoke. Various fights are breaking out, but there is an area of calm in a small room lit by a dim pink light on the far side of the building. You realise it is probably where Mandrake is waiting and that you must visit there before returning to the street. However, as you pass by, a space opens at the bar, revealing a thug of a barman covered head to toe in clan tattoos. His muscles ripple with the effort of slowly polishing a chipped glass. Noticing you staring, he shrugs his shoulders to ask what you'll be ordering. To speak to the barman, turn to **138**. To head past and investigate the small room on the other side of the bar, turn to **179**.

118

You enter the dark alleyway cautiously but are soon washed in a soft green light. It is being emitted by a structure that towers over you, easily eight feet tall and built from solid metal. You recognise it as the MindPod that Mandrake has sent you to destroy. Turn to **34**.

119

You take the **DISRUPTER GRENADE** from your **PACK** and twist the priming dial until it clicks. You drop it to the floor and take a step back, unsure what it about to happen. Rather than a flash or an explosion, a high-pitched whistle fills the air for a microsecond, hurting your ears but nothing worse. The two android guards slump over, all power lost. As they switch off, so too does the lasergate blocking entrance to the core. You race through, counting down the seconds before the effect wears off.

Beyond the lasergate is a covered walkway, protected from the rain by metal arches supporting filthy glass panels. They emit an eerie glow from the layers of unprocessed flux dust that has settled on them over the millennium, giving the whole area the feeling of an underground cave.

The walkway to the core entrance is a few-hundred feet long, and you are barely halfway when the 'droids return to their guard and trigger the alarms. A piercing wail rips through the noise of the machinery and the drones of the people waiting for entry to their shift. A combination of high-pitched sirens and distorted electronic screeches echoes off the concrete, neon canyons that surround you, reverberating until they are a solid wall of oppressive noise.

You push on, every sinew in your body urging you to reach the next doorway before the guards notice you, but you notice a single drone ahead of you, hovering in the air and scanning the area for any movement. You manage to fire off a single shot, hitting it square in the centre. It sways in the air but steadies itself and bears down on you like a wasp. You seem to have damaged its communication circuits as it is unable to call for support, but if you don't defeat it quickly, it won't be alone for long.

You may only use weapons with the **RANGED** keyword during this battle. If you don't have any or run out, you must make an attempt to flee by testing your strength. If you are successful, you make it to the door before the drone can call in reinforcements. It manages to get one final shot into your cowardly back, inflicting **3 HEALTH POINTS** damage. If you take this action, turn to **198** to continue your adventure.

If you fail your strength test, turn to **175**.

DRONE:
Strength: 8
Health: 6

If you defeat the drone, turn to **198**.

120

Eventually, the street comes to an end at a large concrete block of a building. The only way in is a small wooden door down a dark passage to the side. The door itself is hanging from one hinge, but a muscle-bound creature with several heads and and angry look is turning the few people who approach away, not always in a friendly manner. Overhead, a tram carriage glides through the night before disappearing into a station that looks to be connected to the rear of the building.

To approach the guard and try to talk your way into the building, turn to **32**.

To return the way you came, turn to **313**.

121

You leave the ruined shell of the crabman hissing and creaking in the rain and scramble back to the top of the crates. You find an old tarpaulin bundled into a crevice at the back of the boxes and lay it over the barbed wire and the metal grating. It offers enough protection for you to quickly clamber over it and drop back into the alleyway. You head through the door and into the tower. Turn to **87**.

122

The beast doesn't move like a dog. Instead, it flows across the bricks, struggling to keep its balance. It tries to attack with its teeth, but its shape flows strangely with the effort. In the end, it seems to realise that the best course of attack is to lash out with black, stringy tendrils that burn where they touch.

BLACK SLIME DOG:

Strength: 12
Health: 6

If you destroy the hellish creature, you return to the street and explore the empty storefronts opposite. Turn to **58**.

123

The android looks at you for a moment trying to process your lie. It quickly becomes clear that she doesn't believe you. Her mechanical eyes flash, and she flexes into a battle pose. You curse your bad luck and prepare to fight. Turn to **30**.

124

There is a small amount of foot traffic along the street, but people here seem to be

even shadier than those back on the main road through the district. Hushed deals are taking place in every shadowed nook and cranny, and furtive eyes dart past you, never quite settling on you but making sure that you are watched. You soon reach a set of dark stairs leading down into a subterranean hive of noise and a pulsing black-light glow.

To descend the stairs, turn to **220**.

To continue along the street, turn to **231**.

125

You place the helmet carefully on the desk and make your way around the wall of the building until you stop suddenly, the sound of breaking glass echoing from somewhere ahead. You proceed with caution, crouching against the wall where possible. The orange lights make the whole place feel like it's on fire, but the shadows offer a small amount of cover as you approach the source of the noise. Turning the corner, you stop and stumble backwards. Ahead of you is a towering cyborg, over ten feet tall and with the enhanced body of a brutish man. His muscles gleam in the flickering lights and blend seamlessly into the polished metal limbs that have replaced all four of his own. The piston joints move silently over each other as his arms work at breaking down an android for spare parts.

Slowly, you try to edge past him, but your foot slides on a patch of grease, and you crash into the wall. He spins around, his red bionic eyes glowering at you. You spring to your feet and ready yourself for his attack.

BIONIC BEAST:

Strength: 16
Health: 12

If you defeat the cyborg, you manage to wrestle a barbaric saw from his hand. He has been using it to slice through the metal of the android, and the blade is viciously sharp. You may choose to add it to your **WEAPONS**.

BARBARIC SAW:

Strength: + 6
Durability: 6

Once you have defeated him, or if you managed to flee, turn to **56**.

126

The cabinet is a thick steel box bolted to the wall. It is roughly four feet high and half as wide. The door is locked with a cheap padlock that gives way on the second blow from your pistol hilt. Inside, you find an old, dented brass knuckle-duster and a rare PunkBow. You've heard about these fierce crossbows, but you've never seen one. Instead of bolts, they fire a low-frequency energy wave that hits with the force of a blunt brick. Add both to your **WEAPONS**.

BRASS KNUCKLE DUSTER:

Strength: +1
Durability: 8

PUNKBOW:

Strength: **NA**
Special ability: Whenever you hit with this weapon, roll a die. If you roll a 5 or a 6, your enemy is knocked over, and you get a free hit. Deal double damage for this round.
Durability: 10
Keyword: **RANGED**

There seems to be nothing else in the room, so you head back towards the entrance.
Turn to **105**.

127

As you get closer to the crate, you realise that the surface of the metal is moving slightly, as though it has a forcefield protecting it. You recognise it instantly as the newest nanotech. Instead of a forcefield, thousands of tiny **MECH WASPS** surround the object, on constant guard for any intrusion. This kind of tech costs a small fortune, so whatever is inside must be valuable. On the other hand, nanotech is notoriously aggressive. The crate is protected by a retina scanner. If you have **THUNDERGILL'S PROSTHETIC EYE** in your **PACK** that might help, turn to **86**. Otherwise, you must try to force the lock open with force. Test your strength. If you are successful, turn to **159**. Otherwise, turn to **69**.

128

You reach the tram station just as the previous travellers are disembarking and forcing their way down the slippery metal steps. A busy neon sign overhead reads **"CENTRAL LOWER"**, casting the punters in a strange pink light. Each one pushes and

shoves for their own small private space in
the throng. You wait for them to make their
way out into the street before sprinting
up the steps yourself. There is a single
hovertram carriage waiting, its doors open,
and a welcoming, warm light glowing from
inside. There doesn't seem to be anybody
else on board. You figure that there must
be a problem further along the line that is
holding up the service; they never normally
wait in the station for this long.

To step into the warm tram, turn to **6**.

To head back down the steps and return to
the street, turn to **137**.

129

The mech suit groans and powers down,
sending sparks spluttering in all directions
and oil leaking onto the concrete.
Staggering from the wreckage, Thundergill's
body is broken and weak, but he isn't dead
yet. You approach him, weapon drawn,
ready to take the final shot to put him
out of his wretched misery. As you do, he
glances up at you and smiles. You stop,
unnerved by his grin. He winks and tosses a

small metal canister at your feet.

It explodes with a blinding flash, causing you no damage but blinding you for a few seconds. You blink desperately, trying to track his shadowy shape as it dodges away from you. You fire off a few rounds but hit nothing. When your vision finally returns to normal, Thundergill is nowhere to be seen.

You glance around the factory core, but there are no other doors, and the main entrance is too far away for him to have reached. There must be a secret way out of the core, but you don't have time to look for it. If you know where it is, turn to that passage now. If not, turn to **107**.

130

Leaving the dark alley and the esper behind, you step back into the main passageway and head onwards. Turn to **77**.

131

Standing in the shadows of the enormous and sprawling factory, a mesh of rusting metal and pulsing flux, you start to question whether revenge against Thundergill is worth it. The central tower seems to have a force of its own. You get the sense that somehow it is watching you, waiting to see what you do next. Entry into the hive that surrounds it seems to be through a single unguarded lasergate. There is a constant stream of harried, soulless workers passing through it in both directions, but the gate snaps shut after each one. You watch as one broken man doesn't quite make it through in time, and the lasers slice through his body. Immediately, a pair of meat-hoarders scurry out of the shadows and drag the body away to the meat factories. You've heard about them before, the terrible places where bodies are broken down for parts or to feed the hungriest in the slums. You've never believed the rumours until now, but this close to the flux core, anything goes.

On your slow approach to the gate, you realise that the workers are scanning small cards on a pad next to the gate. They all seem to be carrying a pass to allow them entry. If you have any **UNION CARDS** in your **PACK** and wish to try scanning them, turn to **111**. Otherwise, your only choice is to turn back for now.

To return to the crossroads and head along

the dark road, turn to **290**.

To return to the crossroads and head towards the pulsing light and broken-down factory, turn to **98**.

132

Desperate to escape your impending torture, you thrash against the cuffs, finally splintering the bolts that were holding the chair to the floor. You crash down onto your side, your arms still pinned behind you. Test your strength. If you are successful, turn to **52**. Otherwise, turn to **35**.

133

The alley is once again empty except for the noise from the Rusty Pipe and the occasional patron staggering unsteadily back out into the night.

To look inside the storefront marked "Sweeney's Pies", turn to **255**.

If you haven't already, and you'd like to explore the room marked "Archives", turn to **200**.

134

"Can I 'elp you?" The barman towers over you, his face twisted into an angry snarl.

You ask about the poster, but he doesn't answer immediately. He stops in the process of scrubbing the glass in his hand and looks you up and down. "Them's what need to know about the poster, know about it."

It seems that the only way to get more information from him will be to try to persuade him to tell you. If you would like to attempt to persuade him, roll a die for each of you. If your roll is higher than or equal to his, turn to **20**. If his roll is higher, turn to **316**. Alternatively, you can choose to walk away. If you haven't already investigated the small room on the other side of the bare, you can head there now by turning to **179**. Otherwise, you return to the street. Turn to **62**.

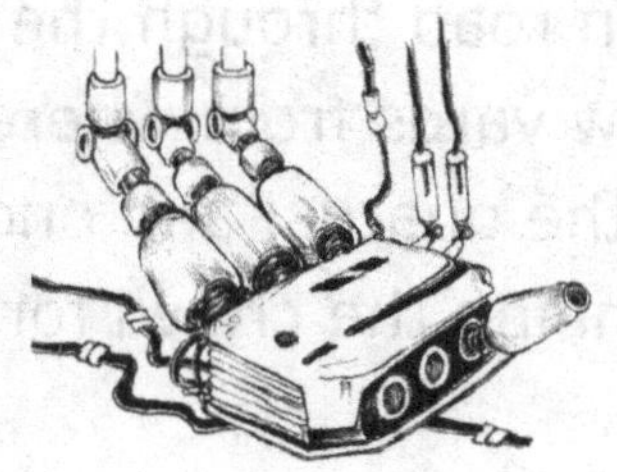

You leave the room as quickly as possible, locating your **PACK** and **WEAPONS** lying against the wall of the corridor outside. You snatch them up and try to find your way out of the building. It doesn't seem to be guarded, but there are glowing cameras in the corners of every passageway. There's no point trying to evade them. Instead, you rely on speed. You try to head away from the room at every corner, and you eventually find yourself at a fire escape hidden behind a stack of old cardboard boxes. You push them aside and hammer on the rusted bar until the door slams open into a dark alleyway. Only the bright neon glow of an advertising board high overhead on the wall of one of the surrounding factories punctures the shadows.

The alleyway is closed off except for a narrow exit at the far end. You shimmy between the walls until you emerge back onto the main road through the district. You are only a few yards from where you were attacked by the guards, and once again, they are scanning the crowd for any rebels. Turn to **230**.

136

You fumble around in the dark, desperately searching for a switch or other source of light. You appear to be standing on a wooden walkway, which is slippery underfoot. You try to use your toes to feel around for the edge but stumble forwards and step into a liquid up to your ankles. You instantly feel it begin to burn through your boots and start to eat into your ankles. Deduct **4 HEALTH POINTS** (reduce your **HEALTH** to **1** if you would otherwise die).

Eventually, you locate a small power switch, which you turn to full power. Several small plasma bulbs flicker into life, casting nothing more than a weak glow over everything. You take the time to quickly bandage your feet before taking in your surroundings. Turn to **205**.

137

You ignore the open carriage, remembering what Mandrake said about avoiding enclosed spaces until the espers have been dealt with. Sure enough, just as you are carefully making your way back down the treacherously slippy metal steps, you are sure that you catch a glimpse of a crimson-hooded figure disappearing into the crowd. Have you just avoided an untimely and gruesome death? Or are you just paranoid in a city filled with betrayal? Either way, you make it safely back down to the street, where you turn your gaze towards the flux tower and make your way into the night.

Turn to **78**.

138

You approach the bar and lean on the metal top, trying hard to ignore the sticky liquids that soak into the elbows of your coat. There's an overwhelming array of coloured liquids on display behind the bar, but you also notice a grubby poster plastered to the wall behind them. You can ask the barman for a drink by turning to **65**, or you can try to get a closer look at the poster by turning to **134**. If you haven't already checked out the small, dark room, you may leave the bar and head towards it by turning to **179**. If you have already been into the other room, you leave the bar. Turn to **62**.

"Why thank you, kind sir," the woman hisses. Before you can react, she slips away into the night, leaving you alone with your thoughts. Afraid of further attacks, you race back towards the steps and descend down to the lower level, where you slip back into the throng of people. Turn to **262**.

The heel of your heavy boot catches against a shard of metal, but you manage to steady yourself before you fall headfirst into the dust. You make it to the rusting walls before the guards notice and begin to feel around for a weak spot.

You soon find a small hole and make short work of opening it up as quietly as possible. Unfortunately, the metal is still sharp, and it cuts into the palm of your hand. Remove **2 HEALTH POINTS**.

Once you have squeezed through the gap, you edge along the wall until you find the main road into the district. You stop and take in your surroundings. Turn to **234**.

141

It pains you to walk away from such beauty, but you know that you need to locate Mandrake and find out what she wants from you. You try your hardest to continue, but each step drains your energy more. If you have anything in your **PACK** to restore any **HEALTH POINTS**, you may use them from this point onwards. Turn to **264**.

142

Time slows until you are focussed only on your breathing. Your finger grazes the trigger, your eyes blink, and your cheek presses against the cold metal of the rest. Thundergill weaves slightly, either through weakness or an attempt to dodge out of your way. You track him easily, the tip of your weapon following him like a magnet. You squeeze, and the recoil kicks back against your shoulder, but you hold firm.

Thundergill collapses forward, a dozen yards short of the platform. Whoever is piloting the ship must be watching because they raise it quickly, and within seconds the ship is rising out of the hanger's skydoors into the sky. Thundergill's body remains limp on the ground. You know instinctively that you made the shot, that your revenge has been exacted.

"You did it," a familiar voice says from behind you.

You turn to face Mandrake. "We did it," you offer as a reply.

"This is just the start," she says, taking you by the waist and leading you away. "The real work begins now."

"What work?" you ask, unsure what she means. "Surely getting rid of Thundergill was the aim."

"We needed him out of the way so that we could rebuild this district to be something better. This is just the beginning."

"The beginning of what?" you ask again, growing frustrated.

"The fall of District-U!" she says gleefully.

Somehow, you can't help but get excited. If she's right, and you can rebuild the district without the tyranny, then perhaps it can once again be a District Utopia.

143

You step back onto the metal walkway and pull your coat around you and your hood up. The rain is heavier than ever, and you barely notice the tall woman waiting for you. "Now, now. What's a low-level dweller like you doing up here?" she says in a deep whisper dripping with an exotic accent. "Let me take you back where you belong. We don't want nothing bad happening to a visitor to our level, do we?" As she speaks, you feel the prick of a knife against your neck. "Of course, my services ain't free," she adds, offering you an open palm.

To pay her 200 **DING**, turn to **139**.

To try to fight your way free, turn to **258**.

144

You feel around on the floor for something to throw, settling eventually on a large metal pipe. You throw it as hard as you can, immediately getting the attention of the cultists.

Roll a die. You must defeat that many cultists in battle.

Turn to **195**.

The doorway leads onto a metal walkway edged with a rusted handrail. It has broken through in places, leading onto a drop to the concrete below. You appear to be inside a large warehouse. You glance back at your cell and notice a tall locker bolted to the outer wall. You kick it down easily and break it open. Your **WEAPONS** and **PACK** are inside, which you quickly recover.

In front of you, the walkway leads out into the centre of the space rather than clinging to the walls. You follow it out, keeping a close eye on the broken grating underfoot. Overhead and continuing to either side is a wide metal ducting. Something is flowing through it, although whether that is air, flux or something else entirely, you can't work out. Several enormous cylinders run from the concrete below to the glass and metal roof high overhead. There are small windows at regular intervals, and you quickly recognise the familiar green glow of flux being pumped through them. This doesn't look like a flux-mining factory, but the large cylinders might indicate that this is a storage facility instead. Other than

a few empty rooms and your cell, there appears to be nothing more on this floor, so you take the staircase at the end of the walkway and descend to the concrete. Turn to **267**.

146

Despite your pain, you are more determined than ever to get into the building. You hastily make your way back along the street until you reach the shadowy steps up to the tram station. If there is a tram station at the back of the building, then it may give you another way inside. You leap into the first carriage that arrives and glance at the glowing buttons.

Choose your destination:

EAST STATION (Turn to **160**)

WEST STATION (Turn to **270**)

CENTRAL LOWER STATION (Turn to **164**)

147

The 'droid takes your card and scans it with a small sensor inside its eye. You hear a low buzz somewhere inside the robot's head, and then a small light begins to flash on its chest. Immediately, the other guard steps forward and strikes you over the head with its steel fist. You feel the crushing sensation of bones breaking, followed by the rough concrete scraping against your back as you are dragged out of the line and into a narrow trench at the side of the gate. The world spins for a second as you are tipped in to join the handful of other corpses already well on the way to rotting.

Before you can crawl out and save yourself, you see a small pack of twisted creatures dressed head-to-toe in dark cloaks gathering around you. They grab a limb each and begin to slide you back out into the shadows, where they will no-doubt haul you away to the meat-processing plants outside the district gates. Your fate is sealed, but thankfully the wound to your head will hasten your demise and mean that you feel no pain as they begin to carve you up for parts.

148

The electric hum of the dying crabs is a sound that you won't forget in a hurry, but you put it behind you and continue slowly along the tunnel. You are wise enough to carry one of the broken shells with you and are able to use the weak green glow to find your way to the tunnel's end. There, you find another set of steps which lead up to an unlocked door. You push through, making sure to close it behind you, and enter a small, empty room. It seems to be a waiting chamber. There is another door on the far side of the room, through which you can hear the sound of laughter. Turn to **317**.

149

There seems to have been some sort of explosion in a building to the side of the road. A large hole has been blown into the front, and several Imperialist guards are lying on the concrete, unmoving.

As you approach the barricades, one of the standing Imperialist guards spots you and signals to several members of his squadron. Their movements take on an increased urgency, and they begin to head towards you in a huddle. You can stick around to find out what they want, or you can try to blend back into the crowd and escape. To stand your ground, turn to **192**. To flee, turn to **230**.

150

You steady yourself with one hand poised to grab a weapon if needed and knock loudly on the door. The sound reverberates around the core, picking up a life of its own, but Thundergill doesn't open the door. You stand on your toes and glance through the window, just in time to see the man on whom you wish nothing more than bloody vengeance climbing out of a window.

Sickened to your stomach, you crash into the door, sending it sprawling into the room and you onto the floor. By the time you push yourself back to your feet, Magron Thundergill is out of the window and climbing into a hovercar piloted by an Imperialist guard. He smirks at you and laughs. "Better luck next time," he screams as the car tilts and begins to pull away from the window.

The rest of the world falls away, leaving only yourself and your grinning quarry. You push hard on your heels, sending your body forward towards the open window. Each step takes you closer, but the car is pulling away even as you reach the opening. You leap, using every last ounce of energy, and your fingers brush against the side of the car. Maybe if you hadn't spent so much energy climbing the steps, or maybe if you'd reacted more quickly, you might have made the leap. Instead, your fingers graze the chrome but can't find a purchase. You seem to float in mid-air for a moment. Time is frozen before gravity takes its toll, and you begin the rapid and inevitable plummet to the ground far below.

151

The doors to the locker are held firmly shut by a heavy padlock. In the gloom and dust of the warehouse, it stands out as being surprisingly well-maintained. It doesn't appear to have been left to the elements like the rest of the equipment in here. If you have a **SMALL KEY**, you may use it to open the lock and turn to **63**. Otherwise, you turn your attention elsewhere. To investigate the broken crates, turn to **300**. If you haven't yet examined the door, turn to **305**.

152

You stagger to your feet and draw your pistol. You know the damage that their electroblades can do, so you try to keep your distance. Unfortunately, they are circling you in perfect formation. The clans were never this organised when you were younger. That's what the Emperor's support will get you. You must defeat both guards, one after the other, before you can continue. They both have the same stats.

IMPERIALIST GUARD:

Strength: 10
Health: 8

If you defeat them both, turn to **79**.

153

You try to ignore the calls from the woman as you wriggle through the window. In your haste, you knock over a jar of prosthetic eyeballs, sending them scattering across the windowsill.

"Hey, those are Thundergill's!" the woman screams at you, dropping whatever she was doing and scrambling around, trying to collect them up. "I can't lose them!"

If it takes your fancy, you may grab one of the eyeballs and hide it in your pocket before leaving. If so, add **EYEBALL** to your **PACK**.

Ignoring her renewed pleas for help, you try to squeeze through the window. It looked wider from the other side of the room, and it has long rusted to the point that it won't budge another inch. Your heavy coat isn't helping, but you eventually drop through and onto the metal balcony. Now that you are on it, you realise that it is a mechanical platform that can be used to raise or lower a worker. You push one of the buttons, and it jolts to life, slowly rising another foot or so. The controls are simple; two arrows, one up, one down. To raise the platform, turn to **269**. To lower it, turn to **219**.

154

Instead of the room that you expected to emerge into, you step through the door and into the dank, dark space. You are underneath an abandoned steel railway bridge, a relic of ancient technology. It forms a short tunnel that opens out onto another street lined on all sides by the backs of factories and other towering blocks of high-rise steel.

"You didn't think we'd have the door at the entrance to our headquarters, did you?" says the small man with a wicked grin and a chuckle. "We're just the guards at the gate. Head on down the street, and you'll get where you need to be going soon enough."

You follow the guard's instructions and follow the alleyway. Turn to **16**.

155

At the top of the stairs, you find another door. This one is wooden, made from old planks strapped together, and is engraved with a name: Mezz Wisten - Mechist. It opens easily, and you step into a small room, dimly lit but with a bright pool of startling white light over a low table. Your entry seems to have startled a middle-aged woman dressed in a long once-white overcoat. Her hair is close-shaved and, until you disturbed her, had clearly been stooped

over the table working. She rolls her eyes
at you and signals a chair in the corner.
On the far side of the room, you notice an
open window, the only source of air in the
otherwise foetid room. From where you
are standing, you can just about make out
an iron balcony on the other side. To listen
to the woman and take a seat, turn to **15**.
To leave through the open window, turn to
153.

156

You approach the taxi slowly, keeping your
wits about you. The driver is giving nothing
away other than his eagerness to speak to
you. His tendrilled arm, wafting the smoke
escaping from his window, moves more
urgently as you draw closer. Somewhere
inside the car, he presses a button, and the
rear door opens. You step back, expecting
somebody to exit the vehicle, but instead,
you stumble back into the immovable body
of a towering guard. You try to turn to face
him properly, but his strong hand grabs
your shoulder and clamps you in place. You
look up into his sunken eyes, dark ringed
and sallow, at the same time as you feel
a sharp pain in your arm and a bolt of

electricity running through your muscles. Tasered, you collapse to the floor, paralysed but awake. You watch groggily as the man reaches down and lifts your body with ease, depositing you in the back of the taxi. You close your eyes and embrace the darkness at the same time as the door slams shut. Turn to **233**.

157

You slide the clasp on the box and gently open the lid to reveal an ornate mechanism. As soon as the lid is open, it begins to spin slowly, setting a group of marble-sized orbs in orbit around each other. The serene movement is accompanied by a tinny melody, obviously created by some ancient mechanism inside the music box itself. Nestled at the bottom of the box is a glass vial. You take it out and examine it, determining it to be a healing elixir. Somebody has scribbled basic instructions on a cardboard label attached to the cap. You try to hold it in the faint glow of the candle to read it and can just make out the scratchy handwriting, but it is indecipherable.

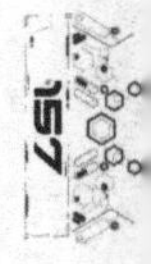

"It'll bring you back from the dead." You glance around at the intrusion into the silence of the room, losing your footing on the ladder. You plummet to the floor, where you land awkwardly. Deduct **2 HEALTH POINTS**.

You add the **RESTORATION ELIXIR** to your **PACK**. If you die in battle, you may use the elixir to return your health to its maximum.

You may try to flee through the red door by turning to **275**.

Otherwise, you may stay and engage with the man by turning to **50**.

158

A powerful flux-chip will be inserted into the base of your skull and wired into your subconscious. Your power over others is unrivalled whenever this upgrade is enabled, and they will find it impossible to resist whatever it is that you ask of them.

Turn to **83**.

159

You smash the handle of your pistol into the lock over and over until the metal is warped and hanging from the crate. The nanobots easily detect your intrusion and swarm towards your hand, biting at your skin where they touch. Luckily, you manage to break the circuitry of the lock before they do too much damage. Remove **1 HEALTH POINT**. As soon as you hear the hum of the electromagnet powering down, the nanobots fade away, and the lid pops open slightly. Turn to **176**.

160

The soft action of the magno-tech system barely registers in your legs as you quickly reach tremendous speeds heading away from the station. From the protection of the pod, the eerie glow of the district as it rushes past is almost peaceful and welcoming. Only those who know the death and desperation that litter each level are truly aware of the truth. Even those who live high amongst the stars are dimly aware of the rot that eats away at the very foundations on which their lives are built. The wealthy and powerful are nothing if not blind to the travails of those beneath them, you remind yourself, even if those problems will inevitably lead to their own ultimate downfall.

Lost in your own melancholic reverie, you are only aware of your destination arriving by the pulsing sound of thousands of people cheering and snarling in unison. You leap from your carriage the moment it comes to a stop and step out into an arena of noise, sweat and blood.

The station is busy with people heading in every direction. Those leaving are angry and covered in blood. Those arriving seem to be filled with nervous energy and are holding thick wads of **DING**. What have you stumbled upon?

Turn to **286**.

161

The crates shift disconcertedly under your weight, but they hold firm enough for you to quickly scamble to the top and drop down on the other side. Tall structures form walls on both sides, and the street ends abruptly ahead of you with a strong mesh fence topped with barbed wire. The buildings on either side rise without any pathways between them, and the torrential rain is pouring into the small square in which you find yourself. A large fire burns in a metal drum in the centre, and a small group of people are huddled around it. They turn their heads and glare at you. Turn to **25**.

162

"I'm glad to see you made it here alive," Mandrake says, offering you the battered leather recliner opposite her desk. You settle into the surprisingly comfortable cushions but remain quiet. "I need something done, and I need it done quickly and quietly. If you agree to do it, it's worth 1000 **DING**."

"What's the job?" you ask.

Mandrake shakes her head. "It doesn't work like that, my wet and weary friend. You want Thundergill gone, I want this little thing doing. You're either with me or you're not."

To ask for half of the payment up front, turn to **182**.

To accept the offer, turn to **202**.

163

Whoever was making the noise outside seems to have fled at the sound of you emerging, and the alley is once again empty except for the noise from the Rusty Pipe and the occasional patron staggering unsteadily back out into the night.

To look inside the storefront marked "Sweeney's Pies", turn to **255**.

If you haven't already, and you'd like to explore the room marked "Archives", turn to **200**.

164

The carriage flies across the rails at a tremendous speed. The only sound is the clicking of the track as it slides into a new position to take you to your destination. The magno-tech system means that the ride is so smooth that you barely feel like you are moving. Within minutes, you see the metal husk of the district begin to slow down through the window before you eventually stop at the station. The doors open silently, and you try to leave, but a blast from a pulse-rifle crashes into the body of the carriage, missing your head by inches and sending you scurrying back inside.

...eney's Pies!
RISE
...TH PIES

You glance out onto the station platform and count four Imperialist guards, all heavily armed with pulse-rifles and flux grenades. If you have any weapons with the **RANGED** keyword, you may attempt to use them to fend off the guards. You must fight all four and defeat them if you do. Because of their heavy weaponry, any damage they do to you is doubled.

IMPERIALIST GUARD:

Strength: 10

Health: 8

If you defeat them all, turn to **251**.

If you don't want to fight them, you can quickly press the button for another station. If you do this, one of the guards manages to get off a quick shot before the doors close, dealing **4 HEALTH POINTS** damage to you.

Choose your destination:

EAST STATION (Turn to **160**)

WEST STATION (Turn to **270**)

165

For a second, the other side of the door is silent. Finally, the voice returns, "Actually, that's a pretty good motto. I wish we'd thought of that one, but unfortunately, it's not right. Sorry for this-"

Before you have a chance to react, you feel a tingling sensation growing in your feet which quickly grows into a painful burn. You look down and gasp as a forcefield of green flux energy creeps over you. With a loud crack, it pulses through your body, and you collapse to the floor. Remove **2 HEALTH POINTS**.

You stagger to your feet and blink away the pain. The pair of eyes are still staring back at you, one spinning aimlessly in its socket. "Can I try again?" you ask. The voice indicates that you may try as many times as you like. They have as much flux as they need should you get it wrong.

Choose your answer again.

"Trust in the crust!" - Turn to **273**.

"Rise With Pies!" - Turn to **45**.

166

Something doesn't sit right as you proceed carefully along the concrete pathway. The channel of sewage that runs along the middle widens as you get deeper into the bowels of the system. You turn a corner and come face to face with a collection of bones scattered across the ground. You spin around to retreat, but a stone shifts underfoot, setting off a rapid sequence of whirrs, culminating in a laserfence firing across the entrance. Beyond the bones, the room ends at a solid wall. You are trapped, with no hope of escape. All you can here is the merry whistling of your captor, slowly approaching and eager to explore their new prey. Soon, your bones will join those on the ground. For now, your fear is your only companion as you await your death.

167

You crash into the door, sending it tumbling into the room and yourself to the floor. Pushing yourself to your knees, you gaze up into the startled look of Magron Thundergill, your arch nemesis and the target of your boiling vengeance. Before you can react, he sprints past you and back out onto the walkway. You stumble to your feet and

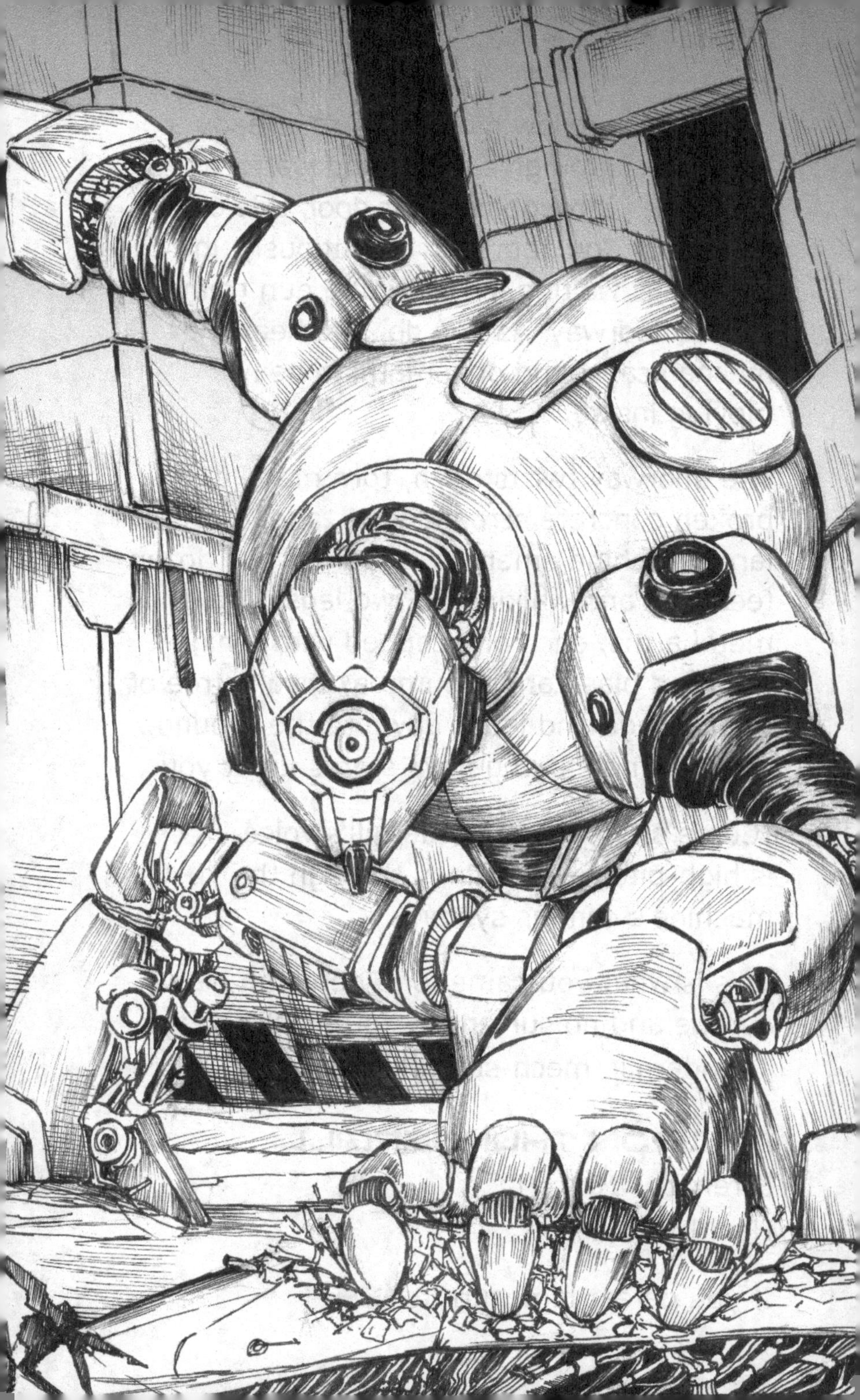

head out to follow him, but he's already a floor lower. You give chase and watch as he pushes through another door, this one darkened. You approach it cautiously, in case he is waiting inside with a gun trained on the doorway. As you do, you hear the mechanical sound of something heavy moving inside.

The doorway twists open, torn metal and broken concrete screaming in tandem. A large machine emerges, towering two dozen feet high and walking on two legs. Two metal arms, each one capped with a high-powered plas-canon, pump as it runs free of the carnage and leaps down to the ground floor. A single orange eye stares up at you.

"Come and play!" Thundergill's voice is high-pitched and tinny through the machine's comms system.

This is what you came for. There can be no escape and no surrender. You must defeat Thundergill, mech-suit and all.

MAGRON THUNDERGILL:

Strength: 16
Health: 20

If you defeat him, turn to **129**.

168

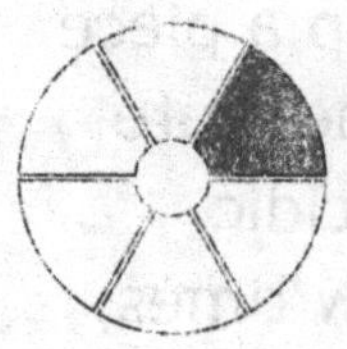

You follow the concrete pathway until you reach a sharp bend. You hear something moving around in the darkness beyond, so proceed with caution.

Turn to **243**.

169

The guards take your card and scan the small microchip. There's a small beep before pages of information flash across their glassy eyes. They stare at you for a moment before waving you through the lasergate and onto the pathway beyond. It is a long walkway, perhaps a few hundred feet long, covered by dark black glass resting on metal archways. The glass itself is coated in layers of unprocessed flux dust, giving it a strange and ethereal glow. You hasten along the path until you reach another door, which you step through into the towering behemoth that is the factory core.

Turn to **49**.

170

Clinging to any last hope, you snap a piece of steel from around the hole in the crate and use it to slice into the black acidic ooze. You manage to catch it a few times, and it pulls away, letting out a shrill hiss as it does. After a few slices, it drops to the floor and immediately begins to flow into the shape of a savage street hound. The damage has already been done to your arm, and the pain is agonising. Deduct *4 HEALTH POINTS* and turn to **122**.

171

Stars pop in front of your eyes with the strain of lifting the heavy door, but you manage to wiggle it up and free. You stagger backwards and allow the door to fall forwards. It crashes through the open doorframe, smashing into the face of an oncoming guard. Before he knows what has hit him, he is carried backwards and out over a railing on the other side of a metal walkway. You gingerly step forward in time to hear both the door and the man hit the floor. There is no further sound. Thanking whichever god seems to be watching over you, you step through the doorway.
Turn to **145**.

172

The factory is boarded up and long abandoned, but you manage to find a doorway that is just about accessible. You pry away a few of the wooden strips and squeeze through the gap. You enter a large space, lit by the grimy glass in the metal roof high overhead. A wide metal duct runs the length of the warehouse, but its use is unclear. Dotted around are several large cylinders. They reach from the concrete floor to the roof and are made entirely of rigid metal. Each one is punctuated at regular intervals by small windows, through which you can see the constant glow of flux. The warehouse doesn't seem to be a flux-mining factory, but perhaps it is a storage facility. Turn to **267**.

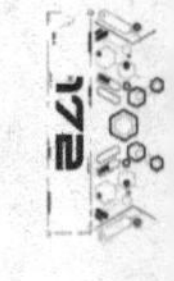

173

You place the helmet onto your head and pull the visor down over your eyes. Immediately, you feel a pulse through the tip of your spine and your vision is overlaid with a strange pattern, almost a reflection of the room around you but slowed down. You wave your hand in front of your face

and watch as it creeps across your vision.
You lift the visor up and check again, but
everything seems normal. Once you lower
it, you again feel the strange sensation in
your neck, and everything slows down.
You work out that the helmet allows you
to tap into the flux network in the district,
effectively turning you into an esper. By
slowing down time, you will be able to
predict your enemy's actions and react
accordingly. Whenever you use the helmet
in battle, do not roll a die for your enemy.
Instead, you automatically win that round
and wound them accordingly. The helmet
seems poorly made, and won't last forever,
so use it sparingly. It can be used alongside
other weapons. You may add **ESPER
HELMET** to your **PACK**. It has a durability of
4 battle rounds.

There is nothing else of interest on the
desk, so you turn back to the room. Turn to
125.

174

You scan the faces of the passing creatures,
trying to find somebody who might speak
your language and who won't hit you for

getting in their way. Eventually, you spot a small, huddled figure, basically humanoid but covered in thick white fur. They seem peaceful enough as they stroll along the road, with none of the hurried attitudes of the others. They are dressed in a simple black coat pulled tight across their chest, but their head is exposed. You step out into the road as they approach and ask them for directions to the Rusty Pipe.

The creature looks at you for a moment before breaking into a smile. "I know of the place," it says in a low but not unfriendly growl. "Not a place for people who are aiming to do good deeds, it must be said. So, I can only assume that dark deeds are on your agenda?" The creature doesn't wait for you to respond before continuing. "Therefore, there will be a cost to you for this information. 100 ding should cover it, I think."

To pay the fee, turn to **41**.

Otherwise, turn to **102**.

175

Whatever damage you have inflicted on the drone is not enough as you feel pulse after pulse of energy crash into your fleeing back, sending you sprawling across the concrete. You barely have a chance to cry out before a final shot to your spine renders you lifeless and ends your adventure here.

176

You flip the lid of the crate open and glance inside. All it seems to contain is a stack of plastic **ID** cards and a small metallic stick. You grab them up and take a closer look. They are union cards carried by the workers inside the factory core. Each one is blank except for a microchip. You add **UNION CARDS** to your **PACK** and pick up the stick. When you push the only button, a short pulse of energy spikes from two prongs on the end. It's a rudimentary Flux taser and might be useful in close combat. You may add it to your **WEAPONS** if you choose.

FLUX TASER:

Strength: +1
Durability: 8
Keyword: **ELECTRIC**

There is nothing else of interest on the roof, so you clamber back onto the moving platform and descend to the street below. Turn to **236**.

177

The barman takes your coins with a snort and throws them into a jar filled with **DING**. You try to catch his attention to ask about the poster, but he's already moved on to the next customer. You down the drink, recoiling at the taste, and decide to cut your losses. The small room is beckoning you, so you head towards it. Turn to **179**.

178

You pull the **LIGHTNING CANON** from your pack and glance down at the vast array of buttons and switches that adorn the console resting above your right hand. The weight of the machine drags your arms down, but your quarry has certainly taken notice of your new firepower. Stopping still, you have a few seconds to figure out how to work the weapon.

There are no icons or symbols that might give you an idea of how to proceed. Perhaps the training that the Imperialist guards go through is enough to teach them how to kill with these things.

Your only hope is to pull the trigger and pray, and so you do just that. Somewhere in the bulky grip of the weapon, a motor whirrs into life, followed by a blinding glow that surrounds you. You feel the rumbling vibrations of a powerful chemical reaction between your fingers and then the sharp pain of thrashing lightning forking out from the end of the barrel. Instead of flying through the air towards your foe, the powerful electrical pulses are grounding themselves on the weapon and through your body.

At first, you feel the prickling sensation of a thousand electrical shocks all over your body, but that is soon replaced by the agony of your blood boiling and your organs exploding under the intense heat. By the time your skin finally charrs and your brain boils dry, you are thankfully long dead. Whether you bought a broken weapon, it had been sabotaged to bring about your end, or you simply didn't know how to use it is irrelevant now.

You head towards the small room and step through a low doorway. The room is bare except for a steel table flanked by four or five soldiers. Each one is dressed in rags of different colours and is holding a battered plasma rifle. Sat at the table is a young woman, perhaps not even out of her teens. She has a narrow face that belies her human heritage, but her dark blue skin and fierce red hair tell you that she is something completely foreign.

"Mandrake?" you ask, offering your hand. She waves it away with a nod and a signal to sit in the empty chair opposite her.

"I know who you are," she says. Her voice is overflowing with repressed anger, and it exudes confidence. "What can I do for you?"

"I actually wondered what I could do for you?" you say, trying to match her confidence and failing.

"Anarchists always need canon fodder," she replies with a smirk. "But you do come highly recommended."

You try not to think about who might have

passed on your name. You prefer to work anonymously, and the idea of somebody like Mandrake already knowing about you makes you uncomfortable. "People don't want to burn down the district for no reason. What's yours?"

"Thundergill." It's all you need to say.

Mandrake knows what it means and nods. "Fair enough." She stands and moves to leave the room. Her guards follow closely. Just before the door, she stops and turns. "You are welcome to join us, but you'll have to prove yourself first. Help us out, and I promise you'll get to watch Thundergill burn. We have a place to lie low, not far from here. You'll have to figure out where. If I tell you, the others will get all snarky. If I were you, I'd keep an eye out for signs." This time she makes it through the door before she turns again. "Oh, and one more thing. You are well-known in these parts. Everybody knows you are here. The espers are particularly annoyed at your return. It might be worth avoiding enclosed spaces until you've dealt with them."

"Espers?" You've never heard of that clan

before. Like your old leader used to say, a new clan is just an enemy you've not fought yet.

"Freaks who can control the wild flux in the Wide using their ESP skills. Dangerous, and they spend most of their time out of their minds. Don't mess with them."

You watch Mandrake slink out of the room and make her way through the brawling drinkers before you make your own move.

Turn to **62**.

180

There may well be more things to explore in the bedroom, but you don't have the energy to risk it. Using what little strength you have, you stagger back out through the door and straight into the arms of Mandrake. Your eyes dim, and the light around you fades quickly. Only Mandrake's cold smirk remains before you drift into darkness. Turn to **4**.

181

"You don't belong here," the man says, "but then, neither do I. My name is Henry. Tea?"

You introduce yourself and accept his offer of tea. It is bitter but not unpleasant, and you feel it restoring some of your health. Add *2 HEALTH POINTS*.

"There are few of us left," Henry continues. "But we are out there, hanging on and leading secret lives."

You explain that you don't have time for a history lesson, that you are on your way to meet a friend. You aren't unkind, but you are all too aware that time is precious.

"I will not keep you long," Henry says with a smile. "I have been watching you since you arrived in the district, and I think you might be able to help me. There was once a book that detailed the history of humanity. It was called The Hubris of Man. I doubt you have heard of it, but legend has it that it contains certain secrets that are of interest to me. You don't need to know what they are, but I would like you to retrieve it."

"There are no books anymore, old man," you snap. You get the sense that he is wasting your time. "They were destroyed by the Emperor hundreds of years ago."

"True, but a digital copy was made, and it still exists. Take this," he offers you a small piece of perspex, an inch on either side. "If you manage to find your way into the district archives, find the book and copy it to this drive. I will make sure you are suitably rewarded."

Even though you are reluctant to take on more problems, you snatch the **PERSPEX DRIVE** and add it to your **PACK**. You bid the man good day and head back out into the rain. Turn to **143**.

182

Mandrake raises her eyebrows and glares. "Fine," she concedes. "But if you want half now, you only get 600 **DING**. 300 now, 300 when it's done."

If you are prepared to accept the offer, add 300 **DING** to your **PACK**. If you'd sooner stick to the original offer, you apologise profusely for any offence caused. Mandrake gracefully accepts. Turn to **202**.

183

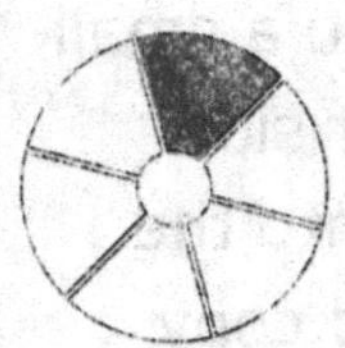 The planks forming the wooden walkway seem to get slowly more rotten as you proceed along the track until, eventually, you are stepping onto them tentatively at best. You follow the pathway as it doglegs right and then left before it finally comes to an end. Ahead of you, there is a concrete pathway that leads to a set of stone steps back up towards fresh air. Between you and it is a jump of perhaps five feet, where the wooden planks have rotted through.

Test your strength. If you are successful, you make the leap and land on the concrete with room to spare. If not, you stumble backwards, plunging your hand into the toxic sludge. You suffer *2 HEALTH POINTS* damage before quickly recovering and bandaging your wounds.

Turn to **218**.

184

Eventually, the alley widens into something that might more reasonably be called a street, which itself gives way to a broad square lined with gritty sand. Most of the land outside of the district is hard, grey desert, but it's unusual to see it within the slums. Even where the houses are little more than sheet metal hammered together, the streets and alleys are concreted. Slowly, you take in the square and realise that it is surrounded by concrete bleachers. They are well-worn and stained, mainly with smudges of dark red and brown. Your appearance in the square seems to have caused a commotion, and people are rapidly filling the seats around you. Turn to **285**.

185

If you haven't yet checked out the door, turn to **305**. To look more closely at the locker, turn to **151**. To return to the corpse for a closer look, turn to **207**.

186

Most of your body is still hanging below the barbed wire and the metal grating, so it will take all of your strength and flexibility to pull yourself through unharmed. Test your strength. If you are successful, turn to **277**. If you fail, you lose your grip and fall through the shredding barbed wire and back into the alleyway, landing heavily on your back. Roll a die. Remove the resulting number of **HEALTH POINTS**, wipe yourself down and head into the tower. Turn to **87**.

187

Upon closer inspection, the door is hanging on a simple set of hinges. Your movement in the cell has sparked interest outside, as you expected. The sound of feet running towards you grows louder, but you still have a few seconds to investigate further. If you grit your teeth and heave on the door, you should be able to pull it up and off the pins that hold the hinges in place. Test your strength. If you are successful, turn to **171**. Otherwise, turn to **293**.

188

Replacing the bones in your hand with a flexible and strong polymer and the skin with modified sandworm hide, the power gauntlet increases your **STRENGTH** by +2 whenever you use it.

Turn to **83**.

189

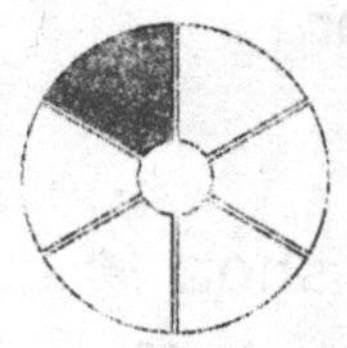

The passageway continues eastwards for a while. The trickle of toxic sludge along the central channel slows until it is nothing more than a film of scum on the concrete. Eventually, you reach a turning that heads north. It seems to be filled with ankle-deep filth. The main passage carries on eastwards, where it seems to lead to a wooden walkway.

To turn north, turn to **274**.

To continue east, turn to **311**.

190

The rusting metal groans underfoot but seems stable enough. You apologise to the young girl who seems startled by your appearance in her secluded hideaway. She calms down quickly and introduces herself as Pygon, one of the newest recruits to the anarchist movement.

"I don't recognise you," she says, taking a sip of a toxic green liquid in a small glass. "Stim?" she asks, offering you a sip.

You shake your head and explain that you've only just started working for Mandrake.

"Your loss," she says, downing the shot. "She won't give you anything big to do if you're new," Pygon groans. "It's the same for all of us."

To explain your mission, turn to **217**. To agree with her, turn to **254**.

191

You approach the gate in the damp shadows of the slum towers. When you are within earshot, you deviate to the left, crouch down and sprint as quickly as you can towards the wall. Roll a die. On a 1-3, turn to **288**. On a 4-6, turn to **140**.

192

The guards don't bother to ask you any questions. It is clear to them that you are in some way linked to the murder of their colleagues, and there's nothing you can say to persuade them otherwise. The first to reach you lashes out with his steel baton, which catches you in the centre of the forehead. You cry out in pain and drop to the floor, where their boots and Flux prods finish off their attack. You feel the cold touch of metal against your wrists, no doubt cuffs to keep you restrained while they take you back to their headquarters. You feel something sharp cut into your arm, and suddenly everything spins, and your head explodes with sharp pain. You close your eyes and bite down on your lip. A final blow to your ribs is enough to knock the air from your lungs, and a strike to the back of your head finishes the job. There is no mercy when it comes to the Imperialist guards, and you receive nothing but their utmost hatred as the rebellious scum that you are. Turn to **284**.

193

You find Pygon lying underneath a pile of metal crates that were knocked over by the blast. She's alive, but you can see that she's badly injured. "Go back to Mandrake," you tell her. "Tell her what we've done and see if she has any further orders. I'm going to have a look around here and try to avoid the Imperialists."

Pygon stands uneasily, using your shoulder for support. "We'll be hiding out at the Mechist's Guild," she says warmly. "Mandrake often meets up there after a mission, and listen to that-"

You both pause for a moment and take in the sound of explosions all over the city. "We're winning," she adds with a smile. "Thanks for giving me an adventure."

"Hey, no worries. Couldn't have done it without you. I'll see you at the Mechist's Guild. Stay safe," you finish with feeling. You feel a deep sense of sadness as Pygon slinks away into the darkness.

"One more thing," she shouts before she disappears around the corner. "The espers will be a lot weaker now. If you feel up to using the tram, you'll be wanting the **WEST STATION**." With that, she's gone, and you are once again left on your own. *Just the way I like it*, you try to convince yourself, but you are less sure of that than ever. Turn to **241**.

Desperately, you try to wipe the ooze from your arm, but it edges away from your touch quicker than you can move. It doesn't take it long to reach the top of your arm, and then you feel the burning begin. Wherever it has touched, your skin feels like it's on fire.

If you have the **POWER GAUNTLET** upgrade and wish to use it, turn to **72**. Otherwise, turn to **170**.

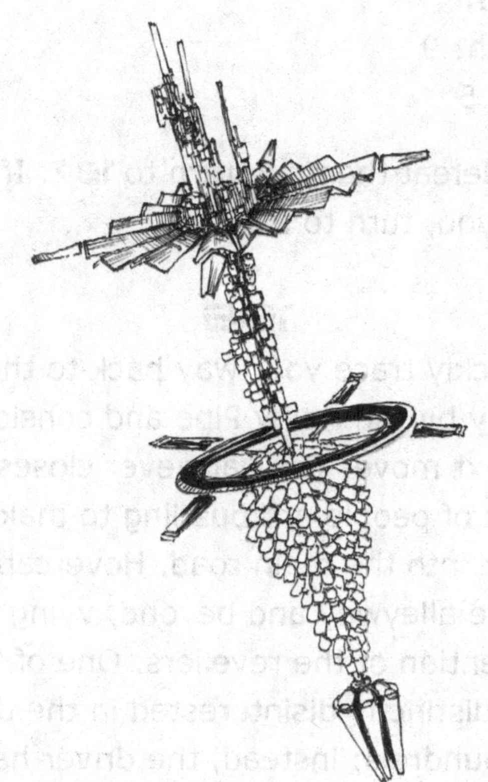

195

Now that the cultists are no longer focused on the fire, you watch the metallic man disappear into the flames, certain that you can hear him screaming. The speed of their attack surprises you, and you barely have time to ready your weapon before they surround you. Each cultist fights with the same stats, and you must defeat them all before you proceed.

CULTIST:

Strength: 9

Health: 5

If you defeat them all, turn to **197**. If they defeat you, turn to **307**.

196

You quickly trace your way back to the alleyway by the Rusty Pipe and consider your next move. The bar never closes, but throngs of people are bustling to make their way out into the main road. Hovercabs litter the alleyway and beyond, vying for the attention of the revellers. One of them seems distinctly disinterested in the drunks and scoundrels; instead, the driver has

his eyes locked on you. His face is hidden beneath a brimmed cap, standard issue for a cab driver in the district, but the cab itself is swathed in a mist of hazy smoke. He leans an arm out of the window and beckons you closer. It's not human, the tendrils and scaled skin give that away, but alien species often find work ferrying scum from one pit to another on the lower levels of the district. Nonetheless, you are cautious about his intentions.

If you are interested in hearing what the cab driver has to say, turn to **156**. To ignore him and join the crowd of people heading away from the bar, turn to **298**.

197

You leave the last body twitching amongst the rusting detritus that borders the street and kick over the burning barrel for good measure. You follow the dark street until you reach an opening to your right. Ahead, the road continues until it reaches a darkened warehouse that rises to the level of the first concrete overpasses. To your right, the street disappears into a veil of darkness. To head towards the factory, turn to **172**. To turn right, turn to **201**.

You waste no time pushing through the door at the end of the walkway, stepping into the towering behemoth that is the factory core. Before you can take in the columnar structure, you are surrounded by several Cybernet soldiers, the personal guards of Magron Thundergill. You've heard rumours that each guard is an ex-clan member, trained on the streets to be brutal and then armed in the most advanced armour and weaponry that money and power can buy. Their armour moves and flexes as they do, giving the impression of scales rather than steel plates. You recognise it as a flux field, a forcefield armour generated by an internal flux battery source. As such, it is vulnerable to **ELECTRIC** weapons. Any weapons with the **ELECTRIC** keyword will deal *3 HEALTH POINTS* damage to each cybernetic soldier.

Roll a die and add 2 to the result to determine how many soldiers you must face.

CYBERNETIC SOLDIER:

Strength: 12
Health: 6

Defeating the soldiers will earn you breathing space, and you may continue to explore the factory core by turning to **49**.

199

The instructions for the machine are simple. When you press the single button, holograms of six dice flicker into vision above a small, early-model holo-pad. The rules are easy enough. You select how many dice to roll between three and six dice. Roll the dice, hoping for different numbers. If all of the dice you roll show different numbers, then you win 50 **DING** for each dice you rolled. However, if two or more of the dice show the same number, then you must pay 75 **DING** for each die you roll, and you win nothing.

You may play the game as many times as you like so long as you can afford to lose. When you are finished, or you run out of **DING**, you return to the street and try the opposite door. Turn to **57**.

200

You pull back the boards and poke your head through the small gap into the dark room beyond. You can't see a lot, so you remove the rest of the boards and clamber through. On the other side, there is an ancient computer bolted to an old wooden desk. The calendar on the wall, complete with artfully posed androids, hints that nobody has been in here for at least 200 years. The screen is dark, and there doesn't appear to be any power to it. Other than the computer, the room seems to be empty, besides a pile of discarded cardboard piled high in the corner. You can hear the sound of something moving about underneath it.

To investigate further, turn to **21**.

To climb back out into the alley, turn to **297**.

201

The road narrows until it is nothing more than a dark passageway between the backs of buildings. The concrete overpasses have given way to metal grating overhead. The sound of thousands of people racing back and forth adds a new layer of noise to the backdrop. Eventually, the alleyway stops at a dead end, but it isn't empty.

Gathered around the decaying corpse of an unlucky Imperialist guard is a pair of creatures that appear at first glance to be large foxes. When they turn their blood-soaked snouts towards you, you see that both have multiple heads and that their bodies are covered with tough grey skin where their fur has matted and shed.

One of them turns a mechanical eye towards you; you hear the nanomotors in its skull whirring as it moves. They aren't full mechanimals, but rather hybrids, an example of their creator's hubris. Whether they were considered failures to be cast out or they managed to escape, they seem to be feeding well on the streets judging by their size and the savagery in their eyes.

MECH FOX:
Strength: 8
Health: 8

MECH FOX LEADER:
Strength: 9
Health: 9

If you defeat them both, turn to **18**.

"We both want the same thing," Mandrake continues when she's sure she has your full attention. "Thundergill is too entrenched. There's no way to get rid of him by the usual means. We have our own *un*usual means, but we need to send a message first."

"What message?" you ask.

"Most of the espers in the city work for him. Whilst they are running around controlling people's minds and exploding their heads and so on, we can't get to Thundergill. Take out the espers, and he's a sitting duck."

"How do we do that?"

Mandrake stands and points to a map of District-U pinned to the wall. It's covered in oil and greasy fingerprints, and the nature of the slums means that no two roads stay the same for long, but it's better than nothing. She points to several sites across the map that have been marked with a vivid green cross. "These are MindPods," she explains. "Together, they form a web of flux wave energy that the espers use as fuel for their minds. They ride the waves and reach out to pull the wires in your head. Take the pods out, and we remove their power."

"There must be a dozen of them," you argue, sensing the job ahead of you growing larger.

"You just worry about this one," she slams her finger on a mark to the east of the district in the shadows of a tram station. "It's near the meat market," she adds. "We've got others taking care of the rest. Deal with this, and I'll know that I can rely on you." She hands you a small packet of putty and an electronic detonator. "Be a long way away when you push that button," she says with a wry smile. Add **EXPLOSIVES** to your **PACK**.

You stand up and nod slightly. "Consider it done," you shout over your shoulder as your head back out onto the walkway.
Turn to **252**.

203

Wretching at the foul odour, you thrust your hand into the rotting sewage that once made up the body of the demon. You can feel it eating into your flesh, inflicting **3 HEALTH POINTS** damage. Just as you are about to withdraw your hand, your fingers grasp a sharp metal blade. You pull it clear of the body and revel in the glow emitting from the blade.

It is a **_PLASMATIC BLADE_**, a very rare and deadly weapon forged hundreds of years ago when the Plasma Knights roamed the galaxy on a quest for peace and justice. These weapons are almost unheard of now, considered a myth by many.

PLASMATIC BLADE:

Strength: +6

Durability: 10

You swiftly add it to your **WEAPONS** and return to the walkway. Turn to **183**.

204

For a few minutes, everything hurts, and the screams of the people in the street are indistinguishable from those in your own head. The sirens of the Imperialist guards as their tanks and heavy-vehicles flock towards you only add to your neural overload. You push yourself first to your knees, where you throw up from the pain, and then to your feet.

You check your body for any damage, but somehow you seem to have avoided the worst of the explosion. A small **_SHARD OF METAL_** has embedded itself into your arm.

You pull it free and add it to your **PACK** as proof of what you did here tonight. Unfortunately, flux shockwaves have a habit of destroying mech upgrades. For each mech upgrade that you have, roll a die. On a 6, that upgrade has been destroyed by the flux blast and is no longer serviceable.

If Pygon is an **ALLY**, turn to **193**. Otherwise, turn to **241**.

205

You are stood on a wooden walkway, a few feet wide and lethally wet underfoot. Underneath it, a thick green liquid oozes slowly towards you. You gather your bearing and note that it is flowing south. Your lungs ache desperately with every breath of toxic fumes, corroding you from the inside out.

*From this point until you leave the sewers, you must colour in a section of the "toxicity level" on your adventure sheet every time to head to a new section. Once you have coloured them all in, you will begin to suffer the effects of the polluted air and must deduct **2 HEALTH POINTS** each time you* *make a decision until you reach fresh air again.*

You traipse along the wooden walkway until you reach a junction, where it continues north, broken in places but otherwise sound. To the east, a concrete pathway seems more stable, and there is less toxic waste flowing along it.

To continue north, turn to **85**.
To turn east, turn to **168**.

206

Your piston legs will increase your speed two-fold. If you are engaged in a battle, and it isn't going your way, you can use your piston legs to flee the scene. Some battles will make it clear that you can't flee regardless of upgrades. If it doesn't mention this, then you may assume you can make a clean getaway. If you flee, follow the instruction for successfully defeating the enemy, but you must not claim any **WEAPONS** or items that you would if you had beaten them.

Turn to **83**.

207

Fighting the rising urger to vomit, you try to move the woman's belongings away from her body with your toe. As you do, something small falls from her pocket. It is a **SMALL KEY**. You add it to your **PACK**. You also manage to loosen a **FLASH GRENADE**. You may add that to your **WEAPONS** if you choose.

FLASH GRENADE:

Strength: N/A
Special ability: When you use this weapon, your enemy is blinded for a single turn. Any damage they inflict on you is reduced to 0.
Keyword: **RANGED**

You return to the warehouse. Turn to **61**.

208

With a heavy grunt, the creature moves to one side and waves you through the door. You quickly step through in case he changes his mind. You are immediately met with a wall of noise and the thick stench of blood and sweat. Turn to **286**.

209

The metal hatch is locked securely, and there's no way to break past it. You can dig around in the trash that surrounds it to see if there is anything of value, or you can return to the street. To dig around, turn to **244**. To return to the street, turn to **263**.

210

The world takes on a pale green hue, distorted by static and strange electrical pulses. You get the sense that you are underneath the old buildings or perhaps even the street itself. There are dozens of small strip lights pushed into the damp cracks between the stones of the walls, but they are broken and smashed. No doubt, street punks have harvested them for the small amount of flux in their tubes. Thin wires trail from one to the other, crackling and sparking with the residual electricity of their unreliable power source.

You reach the other end of the tunnel without incident and climb another set of steps to an open door into a small and empty waiting room. The sound of people chatting and laughing just about reaches you from beyond a further door on the other side. Turn to **317**.

The small man somehow manages to wrestle the brick from your grasp. He tosses it back through the doorway and approaches you, sneering at his victory. Turn to **12**.

"Why are you here?" The taller of the two guards steps closer until you can smell his rancid breath. You turn up your nose and take a step back.

"I'm here to see Mandrake," you demand, trying your hardest to remain cool in the presence of their weapons. You can feel the heat from the barrels where the flux charge is circling, ready to take a chunk out of you if you step out of line.

"Oh yeah? And what if Mandrake don't wanna see you?"

The second guard has circled behind you now, but your senses tell you that he's as close as the one in front of you. The hairs on your neck stand up, and you shiver in reaction to his hot breath behind your ears. "Maybe we oughta have some fun first?" he says, hammering the back of your knees with his foot. Your legs buckle, and you drop to the floor, but you remain calm.

"I don't reckon we oughta melt him yet," the first guard says, looking you square in the eyes. "If Mandrake ain't in the mood to talk, we'll send him on his way however we choose. It'll be nice to have a toy to play with." His wide grin reveals a set of brass-capped teeth and a tongue that's been split down the middle like a serpent.

"Thank you," you mutter through gritted teeth. You keep reminding yourself that the end goal is to speak with Mandrake, not her gutter trash guards.

The second guard grabs the collar of your coat and drags you to your feet. "Come with us," he growls, leading you out of the room. The first guard falls in line behind you, cutting off any chance of escape.

You follow the guard up the steps to the mezzanine floor. The metal grating bangs underfoot, but the guard in the main hall stays asleep. In the far corner, somebody has cut a hole in the wall. It leads into a room that must have been added to the outside wall like a bird's nest. The walls are sheet metal, lined with anarchist posters.

In the middle of the room is a desk made of old scaffolding poles and ancient wood. Mandrake is sitting in a chair reading a handful of tattered papers when the guard drags you in front of her. She smiles at you and waves away the guards. Turn to **162**.

213

The lock clicks open easily. It is clearly well-oiled and often used. You push through the door and flick on the light, which buzzes into life with a pale orange glow. You have found the anarchist's armoury. Weapon racks line all of the walls, although only two slots are currently filled. You know better than to be too greedy, but you assure yourself that taking one of the weapons is only fair if you are going to be helping them out. Choose one of the following, and add it to your **WEAPONS**.

NEURO-DISRUPTOR:

Strength: **NA**

Special ability: This is a small modification that can be added to any weapon you possess. You do not need to roll to use it. When you enable it, it emits a signal that

disrupts your enemy's brain pattern. While in use, your enemy is confused, and their attacks are severely hampered. Any rolls for your enemy's attack are reduced by -4.
Durability: 4

RECHARGE PACK:
Strength: *NA*
Special ability: This is a universal flux-powered charging pack that will recharge any weapon in your possession. Each use of this pack restores the durability of any weapon back to its original count. Unfortunately, any weapons that ran out before you found it have already been discarded, so it may only be used on weapons in your possession now or in the future.
Durability: 2

Once you have made your choice, you leave the armoury and return to the main room. Turn to **76**.

214

The alleyway terminates in a run-down building covered in scrap metal and rusting pipes. Over the darkened door, guarded by a thickset and furry creature, hangs the sign for the Rusty Pipe. From within the building, you can hear the pulsing beat of computer-generated plasmetal. The guard nods as you pass, and you enter the gloom. Turn to **117**.

215

Slaughtering the hopeless virulents doesn't feel good, but you finish off the last with a final strike to their head and shake your head. You pick over their belongings and discover a small **FLUX PISTOL** and some **FLUX GRENADES**. Add them to your **WEAPONS**.

FLUX PISTOL:

Strength: +3
Durability: 5
Keyword: **RANGED, ELECTRIC**

FLUX GRENADES:

Strenth: N/A
Bonus: Automatically remove **2 HEALTH POINTS** from all enemies you have to fight during a battle. Useful for when you face a group. You do not need to roll to win this round of the battle.

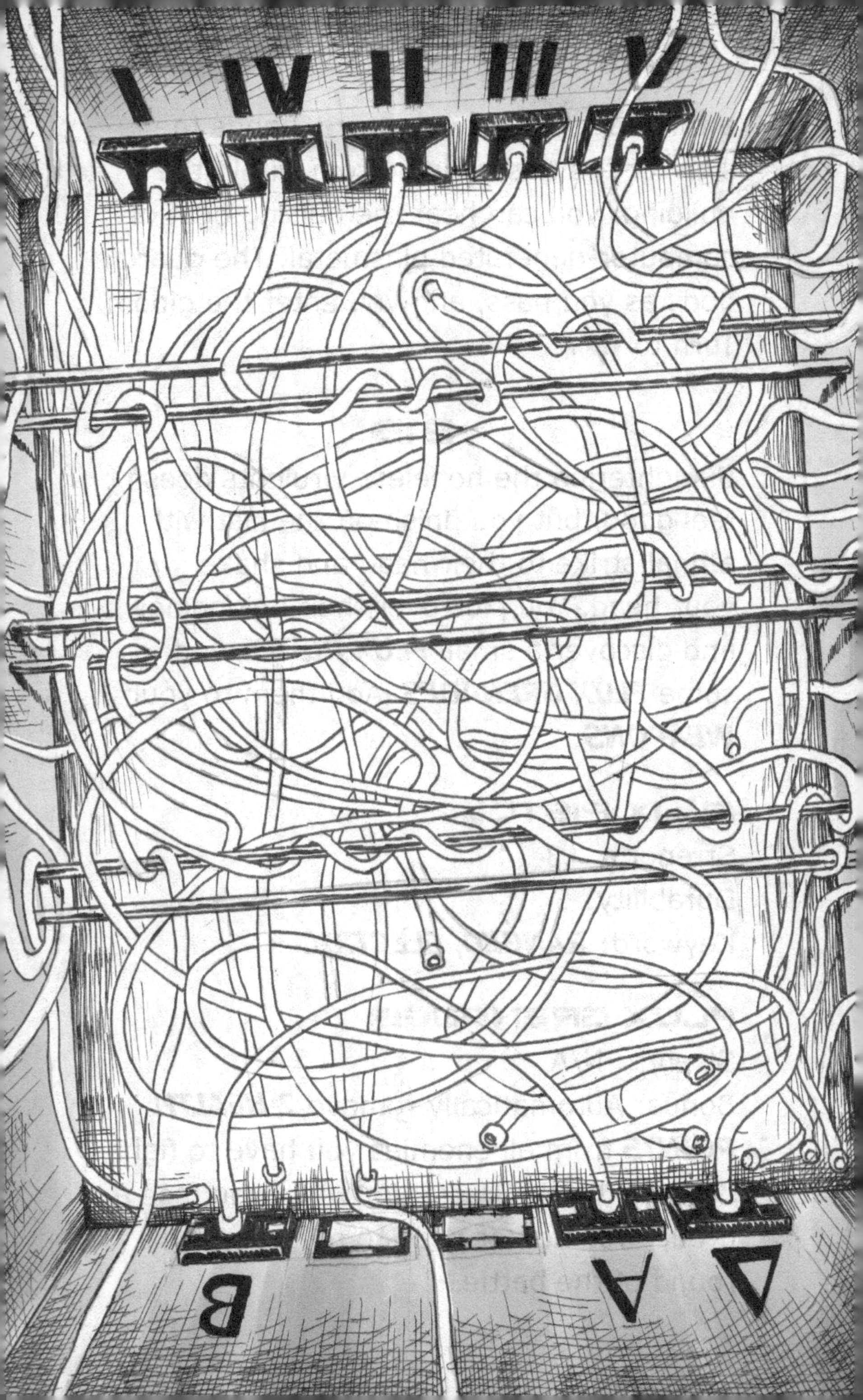

I
IV
VI
II
III
V
B
A
A

Durability: 2
Keyword: **RANGED, ELECTRIC**

You climb back over the pile of discarded crates and back into the narrow side street. Turn to **242**.

216

You stare at the tangled mess of wires in front of you, trying to work out how to approach the problem. You know that you need to cut three wires and rejoin them in a specific way. Each wire is a different colour, although there doesn't seem to be any method behind their design. There is a set of rusting terminals on either side of the cabinet, some of which seem to be connected to those on the other side.

If you know which three wires need to be cut and in which order, you will know which number to turn to now. If you get there and the text doesn't make any sense, then you have chosen poorly. Turn, instead, to **296**.

217

Pygon seems furious that you've been given a mission ahead of her. For a moment, you worry that her bouncing around will send the whole bacony tumbling down into the alleyway below, but you manage to calm her down enough for her to sit back in her chair. "You've got to take me with you," she begs. "Please, I'm useful. I'm great with electronics and explosives. That's how Mandrake found me. I set off a bunch of charges near the flux core. Obviously, I couldn't get that close, but it caught her eye."

"Why couldn't you get close enough?" you ask.

"Only the union workers can get into the core. They've all got cards. If you ain't got a card, you ain't getting in." She looks you square in the eyes and pleads with you again. "Take me, please?"

If you wish to accept her offer, turn to **228**. Otherwise, turn to **101**.

218

You climb the steps as quickly as possible, making sure not to slip on the algae that has collected on the smooth, well-worn surfaces. As soon as you reach the top and burst through a broken wooden doorway, you gulp down lungfuls of fresh air; at least, as fresh as it ever is in the district.

From this point on, you do not need to keep track of your toxicity level unless otherwise instructed.

When you finally feel your lungs begin to absorb the cleaner air, you start to take in your surroundings. You have emerged through the outer gate of the factory into a slum similar to those dotted around the lower levels of the district. Houses have been propped up against each other, nothing more than pyramids of sheet metal and old wood held together with hope. Enterprising individuals have even built small sheds on spindly beams that hang from the outer fences like birds' nests.

There is a steady line of broken souls marching towards the central core, each one nothing more than a shell being put to work until it breaks down and can be scrapped. You can follow them and attempt to enter by turning to **224**. If you'd sooner wait outside a while longer and investigate the slums, turn to **116**.

219

The platform moves at an excruciatingly
slow speed, but it eventually crunches
into the gravel in the alleyway behind the
building. The walls are close together, but
you easily slip through them and emerge
back onto the road that led you here earlier.
You quickly find your way back to the main
road and continue looking for the Rusty Tap.
Turn to **236**.

220

The volume of the music grows
exponentially as you descend into the
darkness of the underground market. A
vast space has been carved out underneath
the district, with a wide-open central space
littered with stalls made from broken
planks of wood laid across rusting barrels.
The walls themselves are peppered with
openings from which strange heads hawk
their illegal wares. No doubt the Imperialists
know that these places exist, but their cut
will be large enough to keep them quiet
for now. Like a nest of hornets, nobody
minds until they break free, and then the
exterminators are sent for. It seems that
this hive of ill-gotten gains will be allowed

to continue for now, so you step further into the madness to get a closer look. The pulsing purple light begins to give you a headache, and the glowing specs of white and neon on the clientele's clothing hurt to look at.

You notice a stall offering some form of elixir and enquire about whether it will help your headache. Even as you speak, you realise that the two-headed woman behind the barrels can't understand or even hear you. With the thumping music drowning out every sound, why bother to learn how to communicate?

The woman proffers you a sample, but you push it away. Without knowing what it is, it's too much of a risk down here. You push on instead and take in the rest of the traders. Most of them seem to be offering small weapons or items of clothing, but a few pique your interest.

As you wander around, you can sense a subtle change in the air, like a storm brewing. Something is wrong, and it's spreading like fire through the tenants of this bleak market. If you choose to take a closer look at a stall, you get the feeling that you will only have time for one before whatever is about to happen happens.

To ignore all of the stalls and make a swift exit, turn to **89**.

To try to talk to the stallholder who is fiddling with broken mech parts, turn to **64**.

To head over to the stall stacked with strange metal packs that look similar to stim sticks, turn to **80**.

To take a detour past the grey-skinned man selling exotic-looking weapons, turn to **38**.

221

Your fingers suddenly feel like lead sausages, but you flex them to get the blood flowing and reach out to grab his card. He rolls in his chair and turns slightly away, but you have it in your fingers and away just in time. You scan the information quickly, but mostly it seems to be a basic **ID** card with his name and a cracked photo of his face printed on the front. In pen, somebody has scribbled the number 213, but there seems to be no other information. You return your attention to the main room. Turn to **31**.

222

The room doesn't yield many secrets,
but you notice that most of the books
are concerned with genetics and mech
modification. You've seen similar titles in
the past when investigating mechists and
their dubious practices. There is a ladder
clipped to one of the walls, so you scramble
up it for a closer look at the top shelves.
The books here are dustier and well-worn,
their spines cracked. There is a strange
juxtaposition between the modern ideas
of mech upgrades and the almost quaint
setting with its candles and paper books.
Halfway down the ladder, you notice a small
wooden box, closed with a small clasp on
the front. You may open it by turning to **157**
or leave it alone and drop back down to the
floor by turning to **303**.

223

You feel a twitch at the back of your neck
and a pulse of energy through your brain.
For a second, your thoughts feel like they
are on fire. You glare at the woman and
instruct her to release you immediately. You
make it clear that your interests align with

hers and that the only way she can achieve what she set out to is by helping you. The words flow from your tongue unbidden, without passing through your brain. There isn't even a moment's hesitation on her part. Within seconds you are freed, and she has taken your place in the chair, cuffed into position and unable to escape. Turn to **135**.

224

The line of bodies heading towards the core entrance has dwindled now that the main shift handover has finished. You hurriedly join the back of the queue and try your best to look as defeated as those in front of you.

It seems to take an eternity for the line to shuffle forwards. You glance ahead and see that each worker is being frisked by a pair of spindly androids. Each one is armed with heavy plas-rifles and polished limbs that could break even the strongest body. There is no way that you could take them in a fight and get out of here alive.

By the time you reach the front of the queue, the weak light of early dawn is starting to wash over you. This close to

the central core, there are no upper levels
to block it out. You stand in the shadow of
the core and stare up. Thick rainclouds still
blanket the sky, but here and there, weak
stars manage to break through for a second
or two, the first time you've ever seen them
in District-U. Even when it was first created,
when the idea of District Utopia was still
more than just a forgotten nightmare, the
stars never shone through the thronging
metal walkways and concrete bridges. You
never saw them as a child, and as a young
adult, your time was spent skulking around
in the dark on clan business.

"Card." The android's voice is clipped
and formal, an instruction rather than a
question.

If you have **VERIFIED UNION CARDS** in
your **PACK**, turn to **169**.

If you simply have **UNION CARDS** in your
PACK, turn to **147**.

If you have a weapon that you know would
be useful here, turn to **119**.

If you have none of the above, turn to
280.

225

The bounty hunter's armour is tightly fitting and doesn't leave much space for pockets. Under one of the plates, you find a small black card. Those with too much money to carry around use these digital devices to store their wealth. Whoever the bounty hunter was, they had money. You scan it with your watch, and it reveals a balance of 3000 **DING**. You swiftly transfer them to your own account and make your way back to the street. Add 3000 **DING** to your pack and turn to **231**.

226

You explain to the android that you are a worker out in dunes beyond the district walls and that you are on your way home now. You try your best to keep your story simple, but it is clear that your captor is unsure whether to believe you. Unfortunately, it seems like it will come down to luck whether you escape unharmed or not. Roll two dice. If you roll a total greater than **12**, turn to **123**. Otherwise, turn to **238**.

You are determined to find the Rusty Pipe and see what Mandrake has to offer, so you head off into the crowded street with renewed vigour. Here, heavy concrete walkways cross overhead like a spider's web. Adverts and clan banners hang from them all, adding to the chaos. The strange darkness of night descending makes the slums even darker than normal, and you struggle to see where you are placing your feet. When you look up, your eyes are bombarded with bright lights and pulsing electricity, but your feet are bathed in pools of black. You try to keep your focus on one level so that your eyes can adjust, and not for the first time, you envy those who can afford cybernetic enhancements. *What I wouldn't give for night vision,* you think, *or even cheap infra red*. Those kinds of enhancements are out of reach for people like you unless you head to the black market. They come with their own risks, though.

While you are trying to make sure you don't trip or stumble into trouble, trouble finds you. You feel somebody grab your arm and place their hand over your mouth before you are dragged into an alleyway formed by sheets of rusting corrugated steel. Turn to **257**.

228

Pygon thanks you profusely. Add her to your ***ALLIES***. Generate her ***STRENGTH*** and ***HEALTH*** the same way you created yours at the beginning of the book. You both climb back through the window and head out into the city. Turn to **196**.

229

Your night vision upgrade will allow you to see moderately better in areas where there is little light. You will be offered the option to use it if it is relevant to the situation. Turn to **83**.

230

The guards glare at you, seeming to recognise you amongst the mass of bodies. Before they can react, you turn on your heels and flee, ducking into the shadows. You press your body against the wall and wait for any sign that they have followed you, but you seem to be safe for now. Turn to **214**.

231

There is little light this far along the street, only the second-hand reflected neon from the wealthier levels overhead. Even that falls in broken patterns as it makes its way through the gratings and past the steel walkways.

"Hey! You buying or selling?" The voice is deep and clearly not human and seems to be coming from a small hatch punched through the corrugated wall of a slum house nestled between two larger buildings.

To approach the voice, turn to **57**.

to ignore it and continue, turn to **301**.

232

The man places his hand on your shoulder and guides you towards a doorway. There are no signs over it to indicate what type of place it is, but you can sense his strength and are powerless to resist.

On the other side of the door, you are led along a dark passageway lined with corrugated steel. The air is damp and smells of rust, but at least you are out of the rain.

At the end of the passage, you are gently pushed into a small, low room. There is an old card table in the centre and a stool in front of a small breakfast bar, but nothing more. The man pulls back his cloak and sits on the floor in front of the table. He is old and looks frail, but you've felt his strength as he led you here. Perhaps most surprising is that he is openly human, the only person other than yourself who doesn't seem to want to hide the fact behind cyborg implants and cheap tech. He implores you to sit with him, and he begins to pour two cups of strong herbal tea as you join him on the floor. Turn to **181**.

233

When you wake, you open your eyes and quickly wish that you hadn't. A sharp pain pierces the back of your head where you were struck, and your eyes feel like they are filled with needles. You wince, blink and try again. You pull yourself up into a sitting position, resting against a cold wall. You are dressed, but your **PACK** and **WEAPONS** have been taken. Until you retrieve them, you will only be able to fight with your fists. You suffer a **STRENGTH** -2 effect until you

are told otherwise. You are also alone. Any
ALLIES that you may have acquired are lost
to you now, either killed or in hiding. Your
poor decisions have come back to haunt
you.

You are being held in a small room, empty
except for a rusted metal sink and an
equally ancient bucket in the corner. Neither
looks like they're worth using. A single
light on the far wall provides all of the
illumination, and that is barely enough to
see by. There is a small window high up in
the wall, barred and dark. Not even a flicker
of neon manages to make its way through
into your cell. There is a door opposite you,
made of solid metal and windowless.

You are under no illusion that you are being
left alone. Somebody will be watching and
waiting for you to stir. You realise that your
next move will be critical. Right now, they
probably know that you are awake but that
you are still stunned and groggy. As soon as
you move, they will be forced to make their
next move.

Looking around, a few things catch your
attention. One area of the wall appears to

be different to the others, as though some of the mortar has been dug out from around a couple of bricks. The other thing is the door. It doesn't seem to have been built as a cell door; instead, it looks like a normal door that has been fortified.

To investigate the bricks, turn to **114**.

To look more closely at the door, turn to **187**.

234

Inside the walls, the district is even hotter. The towering flux mine in the centre of the district generates enough heat to power the entire area, but it also leaks enough energy to raise the air temperature for miles around. The vivid green glow of the flux being pumped up the central column isn't visible from where you are, but you recognise the dim parlour it casts over everything, even this far down in the slums. Wires and washing lines are strung across every alleyway, though nobody has any clothes out to dry. There's no point. What doesn't get soaked by the rain would get stolen in seconds. Instead, they are littered with the detritus of a run-down society; old boots, scraps of metal and litter, and even the odd corpse. There's no law down here, only that which the clans enforce themselves. This close to the wall, the area is crisscrossed with different symbols, none of them truly laying claim to the area. Not that it matters. Your own clan is long gone. You're an outsider who runs the streets. You've got no friends here, none anywhere in District-U.

You shrug against the rain and press on, determined to make it to your rendezvous before nightfall.

Turn to **94**.

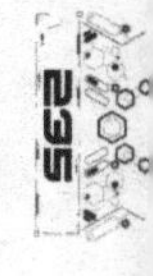

235

Just as you reach the foot of the steps, a voice shouts out from the crowd and identifies you as an enemy of the Emperor. You ignore the cries for you to halt and sprint up the steps until you step out into the foetid air of the district. You take a split-second to decide which direction to head in, which turns out to be too long. A heavy hand grabs you by the neck and forces you into a narrow passage flanked by concrete walls and the rotting corpses of long-dead vagrants. You break free just as a sharp blade flashes past your stomach.

You turn and take the form of the person standing in front of you. They are at least a head taller than you but dressed entirely in red-plated armour. A reflective visor covers their face, and their formless body makes it hard to work out whether they are human or not. With the weaponry they are carrying, it hardly seems to matter.

"You are worth a lot of money to me," the creature says, approaching slowly. "Thundergill wants you alive. He's offering 100,000 **DING**. On the other hand," the bounty hunter swings a blade towards your face, but you easily duck out of the way, "he's also offering 80,000 if you're dead. What's 20 grand between friends?"

BOUNTY HUNTER:
Strength: 14
Health: 10

If you defeat the bounty hunter, you may search their body before heading back into the street. To search them, turn to **225**. To leave the body and return to the street, turn to **231**.

There is more traffic this far along the main road. The soft hum of electric bikes and heavily armoured cars float past, although most of them are taking the higher levels. It's only those that have a business to attend to in the depths of depravity down here that stick to the roads. Every now and then, the clan warfare spills out of the alleyways and onto the streets, and the Imperialist clan make sure they are there to mop it up. Something has happened up ahead, and the road has been blocked off with enormous concrete barriers. Each block is defended by an Imperialist guard, their gold armour flickering neon. If you wish to investigate what has happened, turn to **149**.

To the left of the blockade, you notice a narrow alleyway. Several people stumble out as you watch. Each one has clearly been imbibing significant quantities of alcohol. To take a chance on it leading where you need to go, turn to **214**.

237

The red door swings open easily, and you step into a darkened room. The pulsing light of the city behind you picks out the edges of objects in pinks and blues. You enter further, closing the door behind you so that you aren't silhouetted against the street. On a table opposite you, a small candle splutters in a tall glass jar. It's surrounded by a viscous liquid, a safety precaution necessary because of the stacks of dry books that line every wall. Seeing something as old-fashioned as a candle is a shock, and you begin to wonder what type of establishment this is. Wires hang from the ceiling. Some of them pulse with unseen energy flowing through them. A device made of copper balls and brass filigree spins slowly on a shelf above your head.

There doesn't seem to be anybody about. The room is tall and square, with few places to hide. However, you are filled with a deep unease about this place. It seems to be the home of somebody indulging in dark powers. You can turn and leave by turning to **275**, or you can push on further into the room by turning to **222**.

238

Whatever processing logic is ticking over inside the droid's head, it quickly becomes clear that she believes your lie. Before she has time to question you further, you push past and disappear into the crowd on the main road. Turn to **28**.

239

You are met with a set of concrete steps that rise up towards the centre of the narrow building. The staircase is flanked on both sides by dirty concrete walls plastered with old fliers and clan graffiti. A dim, low-wattage bulb hangs on a bare wire far above you; only the barest glimmer of light illuminates your path. The top of the stairs is lost in a pool of shadows, but you can hear the sound of noisy machinery up ahead. It sounds like it might be a buzzsaw or a drill, or something similar. You glance back over your shoulder, but the door has slid shut behind you, and there doesn't seem to be a way to reopen it. Turn to **155**.

240

Mandrake's nod to the guards in the room is almost, but not quite, imperceptible. You realise what it means in time to hobble out of the room, but the first flux pellet hits you in the shoulder before you can turn into the corridor. It knocks you forward into the railings at the edge of the mezzanine platform. You cry out, but the pellets pepper your body, sending you crashing to the concrete below. You barely live long enough to appreciate the excruciating pain of your broken bones and punctured skin, but you do catch one final glimpse of Mandrake's sad eyes staring down at you from above. Whether Thundergill is defeated or not is no longer in your hands. You have failed.

241

Behind you, the sounds of the Imperialist guards draw closer. The milling crowd should keep them at bay for a while, but you sense that it would be a good idea to move on swiftly. You chase the narrow alleyway until it emerges into a small opening, nothing more than a courtyard stuck behind the backs of several tall buildings. On one side, a stairwell leads up into a stone building. A busted neon sign above it reads: **CE TR L UPPE** , but none of the lights are working, and several letters have long since been stolen away. On the far side of the square, another passageway leads off to the right. It looks to be wider than the one you've left but just as empty.

To climb the steps, turn to **75**.

To follow the passage, turn to **124**.

242

The narrow alleyway diverts to the right after a hundred yards. You follow it and reach a dead-end. There are doors on both sides of the street, both of which appear to be unlocked. One has a crude drawing of a mechanical eye above it, and the other is unmarked. You can just about hear the sound of arcade machines behind it.

To enter the unmarked door, turn to **53**.

To head through the door marked with a mechanical eye, turn to **97**.

To head back to the main road through the district, turn to **236**.

243

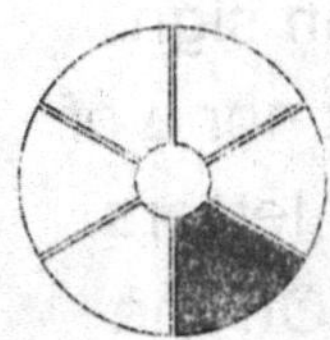

You step into the shadows. You hear the noise again, this time louder than before. Before you can retreat, a crazed woman leaps out from a recess in the wall. Her eyes are wide and bloodshot. Thick green tears drip down from the end of her nose. Her skin is blistered and weeping, her hair chopped into small tufts where it remains. Her mouth hangs open, and her loose teeth fall to her feet as she growls and sneers at you. She seems to be having trouble standing upright. Instead, she drops to all fours whenever she wants to approach. Ending this poor wretch's life could be seen as an act of mercy, but she is swift and strong, so running from her won't be possible.

SEWER HAG:

Strength: 14
Health: 10

If you defeat her, you flee in the only direction possible, heading north until you reach a junction.

To head north along a wooden walkway, turn to **23**.

To head east and follow a concrete pathway, turn to **60**.

244

The rotting garbage that is piled up against the metal fortification yields nothing of value, but as you get closer to the concrete beneath, you notice a manhole cover. It isn't locked, so you lever the lid open and stare down into a dark abyss. You consider your options for a short second, but the sound of guards approaching in the distance makes your mind up for you. You scramble down the rusting pegs that serve as a rudimentary ladder and drop into a dark tunnel. Turn to **8**.

245

"I don't want to be this close to you again," the barman snaps, lifting you by your collar and tossing you back into the crowd.

As you turn away from the bar, you catch a glimpse of the poster and notice a cartoon outline of a steaming meat pie, with the words "Rise With Pies" just about visible behind the grime.

None-the-wiser, you leave the bar. If you haven't already, you can check out the small room at the back of the building by turning to **179**. If you've already been there, you return to the street. Turn to **62**.

246

Pygon steps up to the box and pushes you aside. "Told you I'd be useful," she says with a smirk, following it with a shake of her head and a mocking laugh. "They call these things secure? Honestly, a baby could destroy this."

You ignore her insult and watch over her shoulder as she cuts through several wires and begins to twist the ends together in a new way.

"Listen," she says over her shoulder, "when I connect the last wire, we've got about a minute before this thing goes bang in a big way."

"What's going to happen?" you ask, trying to spy the best escape route.

"I'm adding an alternating relay command into the flux pump array module." Pygon notices the blank look on your face. "Basically, the pumps will switch direction quickly and often, like, thousands of times a second. The flux will be pushed back against itself, creating a superheating situation. Anyone who knows anything about flux knows that you don't get it hot. Once it gets too hot-" she uses her hands to simulate a massive explosion. "Ready?" she asks. "Once I say, we head that way," she points towards an even narrower alleyway. "Get behind something if you can, or just keep running."

Without waiting for a further nod from yourself, Pygon twists the final two wires together.

The MindPod immediately begins to emit a deep hum and starts to vibrate and groan. You feel Pygon grab your shoulder and drag you away before you finally come to your senses. You squeeze into the alleyway and dive behind an old, burnout transport vehicle just as the world around you is ripped apart in a pulsing torrent of green light, a powerful shockwave and then darkness.

Turn to **204**.

The rotten floor groans under your weight, and more than once, you have to leap aside as a plank drops through to the alleyway below. Eventually, you make it to the weapon and reach out to grab it. It flickers slightly under your touch, and your fingers pass through it without resistance. It's a hologram designed to lure foolhardy and greedy thieves into what you quickly realise is a trap. You turn back towards the door where Mandrake is standing, shaking her head, her mouth twisted with disappointment.

You open your mouth to speak at the same time as the floor opens up beneath you. You plummet through the air for less than a second, but the force of the concrete against your spine crushes the air from your lungs. All pain ceases as the nerves in your body shatter, and the electrical impulses misfire and fade away. This is where your story ends, alone and broken in a damp alleyway, a victim of your own greed.

Just as you are beginning to worry that you might never leave the comfort of the chair, Mandrake bursts through the front door with Pygon in tow. "We did it!" she screams, rushing around the room, hugging everyone in turn. Pygon throws you a knowing look, and you smile back at her. "We *all* did it," Mandrake adds, glancing in your direction. "You're one of us, now. You've definitely proven yourself, and I need to repay you."

Mandrake strides towards you, fiddling with a black card as she does. She swipes it over your watch, and you note the **DING** entering your account.

If you insisted on half of the payment upfront, add another 300 **DING** *to your* **PACK**. *If you accepted the original offer, add 1000* **DING** *to your* **PACK**.

"Thundergill is weaker than he'll ever be," one of the voices says, urging the others to their feet. "What are we waiting for?"

"It's not that easy," Mandrake explains. She encourages you all to sit as she speaks, and you gratefully take the opportunity to slink back into your chair. "Thundergill is hurting.

His esper guards are powerless now, but he's not weakling himself. He's still holed up in the central column of the factory, which is unreachable for most of us. There's no way to storm him without him seeing us coming."

"So what? If he sees us, we just cut him down and get rid of him," the voice adds. You nod your head in agreement. Anything to get rid of Thundergill is fine by you.

"He'll escape to the hangar outside of the district walls. There are tunnels everywhere underneath the factory."

"So, what's the plan?" you ask, breaking your own silence.

"We try to gain entrance in a small team. I want you to go," she says directly to you. "I'll send some of my best fighters to help you."

You figure that you've come this far, and getting revenge on Thundergill is your only focus now. You nod in agreement.

Mandrake points to two figures propped up against the far wall. One is a young girl who barely looks to be into her teens, and the other is a wiry man twice as old as you but with the weary eyes of somebody who has laughed at everything the universe has had to throw at them. The young girl seems to sense your concerns, but before you can say anything, she seems to fly across the room and has the point of a blade pressed into your ear.

"She'll do," you squeak, finally breathing as she flashes you a smirk and retreats back to her position on the other side of the room.

"This is Proppo and Thorn," Mandrake adds, indicating Proppo as the old man and Thorn as the young girl.

Add Proppo and Thorn to your **ALLIES**.

PROPPO:
Strength: 13
Health: 10

THORN:
Strength: 15
Health: 9

If **PYGON** has fought alongside you before, you may also add her back to your **ALLIES**. If you haven't, then she is reluctant to trust you now and will remain with Mandrake at the hideout.

Turn to **88**.

The Mad Mechist offers you a seat in a firm but comfortable leather chair. You accept his offer, relieved to take the weight off your feet for a while. He doesn't sit, preferring instead to pace around the room as he speaks.

"Magron Thundergill is a menace. All of this," he points at his own modified body, "disgusts him. He wants to ban all mech modifications in the district. Of course, he didn't feel that way when he came begging on hands and knees for me to upgrade him. Like a fool, I did it. He had everything that I could throw at him. You think I look like a mutant? Thundergill is worse. And he's strong." The Mad Mechist shakes his head in despair. "He's so strong. On your own, you'd have no chance of defeating him. But, I can help."

"How?" you ask, not liking the sound of a modified Thundergill. You wonder if Mandrake knows about this, or is she heading into a massacre?

"All mech upgrades need powering. Some of the older black market ones can be powered by the body alone. More modern ones use the flux-field that surrounds us all. It's especially strong near to the core."

"Thundergills are powered by flux-field?"

"Yes, and no. He was worried about interruptions to the field. With good reason, as well. He controls a lot of espers, but they have the power to control the field. If they decided to betray him...let's just say they could kill him in an instant. No, he wasn't content with the standard power options. He demanded I fit him with his own personal flux source. It's a small orb that he carries around on his belt. It powers everything inside him. If you want to defeat him, you'll have to destroy that."

"And that'll kill him?" you ask, seeing the light at the end of the tunnel.

"No. That'll turn off all of his mech upgrades. He's mostly mech now, so he'll be weak enough to attack. That's your only hope. If I were you, I'd find somebody who can take it out while you distract him."

You sit and think about the new information. If the mechist is right, and you've no reason to believe that he isn't, then revenge just got a whole lot harder.

"Before you go, let me give you something that will help." Before you can react, the Mad Mechist lunges at you, pressing his metallic hand into your chest and pinning you to the chair. With his free hand, he produces a large syringe filled with what looks like a swirling black fog. You try to push him away, but he's too strong. You scream in pain as the needle pierces your skin and the gas pours into your bloodstream.

"Wait," the mechist commands when you try to stand. You soon see why. Sickening dizziness engulfs you. You lean over the edge of the chair and wretch.

"What was that?" you wheeze when the effects finally wear off.

"Nanohide," he replies. "Look."

He points at your skin, which you now see has a faint black haze over it. You try to press a finger into your arm and watch the microscopic nanobots gather immediately. Before you can feel the pressure, your finger is repelled.

"It's like your own suit of armour," the mechist says with a smile.

"Thanks, I think." You stand and shake the mechist's hand. With nothing else to say, you exit through the red door and head back into the street. When you reach the junction, you continue straight, following the road around the bend.

Make a note that you now have the **NANOHIDE** mech upgrade. This increases your **STRENGTH** by +2 at all times. This high-quality upgrade doesn't fail, so there is no test required to use it.

Turn to **268**.

250

Neither of you is in a fit state to fight, but it seems that there is no other way out of this. Roll a die for each of you. If your number is higher or they are equal, turn to **112**. If the guard's number is higher, turn to **48**.

251

Before anybody else can react, you race out onto the platform and snatch up the nearest **PULSE-RIFLE** that you can grab. You also manage to collect a few **FLUX GRENADES** before fleeing back into the carriage and hammering on the buttons to close the doors.

PULSE-RIFLE:

Strength: +3
Durability: 5
Keyword: **RANGED**

FLUX GRENADES:

Strenth: N/A
Bonus: Automatically remove **2 HEALTH POINTS** from all enemies you have to fight during a battle. Useful for when you face a group. You do not need to roll to win this round of the battle.
Durability: 2
Keyword: **RANGED**

Choose your destination:

EAST STATION (Turn to **160**)

WEST STATION (Turn to **270**)

252

Leaving the room, you notice another set of stairs on the far side of the mezzanine walkway. It leads up to a second balcony of metallic grating that hangs to one side of the wall. To explore, turn to **42**. If you'd sooner head straight back out into the sprawl and get to work on Mandrake's mission, turn to **196**.

253

You hear the man grunt something about helping you as you shove him out of the way, but you ignore his pleas and head for the steps as quickly as you can without drawing attention to yourself. The stranger doesn't seem to be following you, and he hasn't called for help, so you scurry down the steps and try to blend in with the crowd on the lowest level. Turn to **262**.

254

"Sucks, doesn't it?" Pygon moans, happy that you're as undervalued as she is. She stands up and climbs back through the window. "If you ever do get any cool jobs, let me know. I'll help you out," she says before she disappears. You give her a moment to leave before climbing back through the window yourself. You head back down the steps and out into the city. Turn to **196**.

255

The smell of stale pastry hits you like a hammer the moment you drop from the window sill and into Sweeney's Pies. On one side of the room, there is an old display cabinet filled with the day's offerings, or at least those on offer on the day that the massacre happened. Evidence of bloodshed is all over the floorboards and the walls, with some bits rotting as they hang from the light fittings. Whatever explosive event happened here, it was swift and terminal. You try to hold your breath against the rancid aromas of death and mouldy crust.

You are relieved to see that there is a door on the far side of the room that seems to be ajar. You sprint over and push it open, taking a deep breath of the slightly less rank air on the other side. It leads onto a dark staircase that descends rapidly. If you have a night vision upgrade and wish to use it, carry out any tests now. If you successfully turn it on, turn to **210**. Otherwise, turn to **2**.

You follow the alley and reach a dead end. To the right, the steel-clad wall of a processing plant blocks out nearly all of the light from the surrounding city. Halfway up, a broken billboard flickers, the pixelated face of the **CEO** twisting and fading as he recycles an old prayer to commerce. Ahead of you, a concrete wall rises perhaps twenty feet before giving way to lethal barbed wire and steel spikes. On your left is an old concrete tower. Its square base has been added to with corrugated metal lean-tos and flimsy platforms at various levels. Whilst it was once home to thousands of individuals crammed into enough space for a hundred, it now seems to be abandoned. There is a small door that seems to open into the ground level. Somebody has carved a crude representation of a pie into the paintwork, a more wholesome companion to some of the other graffiti that has been added over the years.

To scale the wall ahead of you, turn to **68**.

To open the door and step into the tower, turn to **87**.

Stood in front of you is an android, easily eight feet tall and designed to look like a beautiful woman. The porcelain face and exquisite curves are only ruined by the exposed wires and mechanical joints that betray it as a cheap but effective service droid. You've seen them before, working away as waitresses or maids, performing whatever services their wealthy owners require of them. You've never seen one this low down in the district before.

"What do you want?" you demand, feeling the weight of your pistol in your pocket.

"I must take you to my master," the droid responds. Her voice is mechanical but human enough to be slightly unnerving. "He has demanded that you meet with him."

"Who is your master?" you ask.

"That is unimportant. For now, you must come with me."

There is something about the robot that unnerves you. You have no intention of travelling with her to visit some unnamed master, so your options are limited.

To try to persuade the android that she has the wrong person, turn to **226**.

To fight your way free, turn to **30**.

258

You turn to push the woman away, drawing your gun as you do so. You aim for her head but stop short of pulling the trigger. She flickers and disappears, her hollow laughter echoing slightly as her hologram vanishes. You curse yourself for being so frightened, but holo-tech is growing more real every day. The prick of the knife on your neck was real enough; a small electric pulse against your nerves. You take some solace in the fact that it wouldn't have been able to do any real damage, though.

More desperate than ever to meet up with Mandrake, you return to the steps and descend back to the lower level. Without looking back, you blend back into the crowd. Turn to **262**.

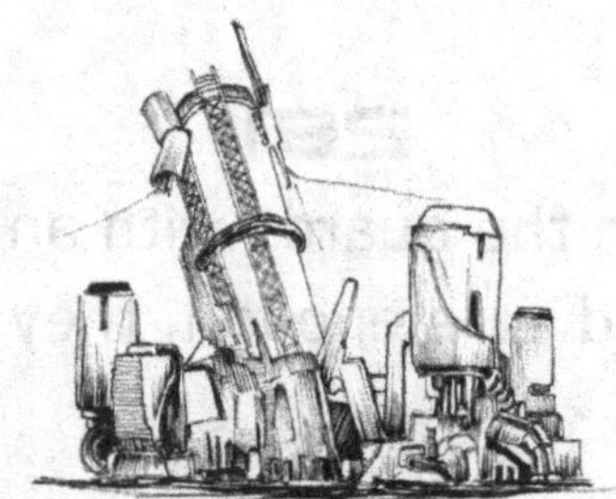

259

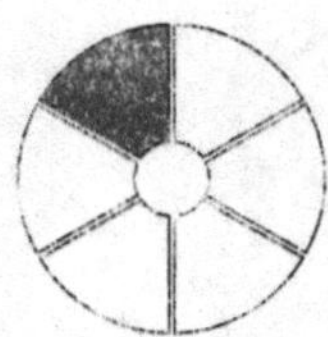

The pathway terminates at a two-way junction. The skeleton of a previous hapless adventurer lies forlornly against a wall a few steps along the southern passage. To the north, you see can nothing but endless concrete. The stench is worse here, and the steady flow of toxic waste seems to increase with every step.

To head north, turn to **59**.

To head south, turn to **166**.

260

The guard stirs slightly as you approach him, but he doesn't wake. He's clearly drunk but alive. You approach as quietly as you can and notice an **ID** card hanging from his belt. You decide to move in for a closer look, but you'll need luck on your side if you are to avoid waking him. Roll a die. On a 5 or a 6, turn to **221**. Otherwise, turn to **13**.

261

You approach the guards with an air of authority, and sure enough, they barely glance in your direction as you walk past and into the hive of the district. When you are several steps past them, you stop and take in your surroundings. Turn to **234**.

262

Even though the main road through the slum is wider than most, there is little natural light down here. The incessant flicker of neon and the blare of advertising signs gives a certain mystery to the gloom, but it's easy enough for you to blend into the crowd. Your heavy coat and deep hood help, but mostly the citizens have learned to keep themselves to themselves unless they mean others harm.

You stop by a particularly vivid sign advertising a new holographic tourism company and duck under an awning to gather your bearings. You try to find any sign of the Rusty Pipe, but down here, there are no street names. If you don't know where you are going, then you don't deserve to get there.

None of the passing crowd seems interested in you, but you may be able to stop one of them to ask for directions if you choose.

Will you ask somebody for directions (turn to **174**), or will you continue searching on your own (turn to **227**)?

263

You return to the darkened street and turn towards the broken-down building. It seems to be your only other option, so you make your way forwards. Turn to **291**.

264

Where the two walls of the tower meet, another hole has been hammered through the concrete. It opens onto another room hanging from the corner of the building. This one's lined with sheet metal, but somebody has at least made an effort to pin posters to the walls. Mandrake is sitting alone at a desk made from metal pipework and rough-hewn timber. She looks up at you and smiles.

If you have a *GET-WELL CARD* in your *PACK*, turn to **74**.

If not, turn to **162**.

265

You lift the woman's dead body onto a spare table and cover it with a sheet. You spare a second to consider the patient currently lying under sedation on the other table, but there's nothing you can do to seal up their wounds. Instead, you push it from your mind and head back to the street. You make your way to the main street and continue searching for the Rusty Pipe. Turn to **236**.

266

You scurry down the steps like the cockroaches that infest the walls and emerge, blinking onto the street. You turn and head back to the main road and search for the Rusty Pipe. Turn to **236**.

267

You wince every time your heavy boots echo on the solid concrete, but you appear to be alone in the building. It's possible that whoever else was in here has hidden at the sound of your arrival. Either way, you don't wish to spend any longer here than you need to. Whenever the warehouse was abandoned, the occupiers seem to have emptied it thoroughly; either that or it has been stripped bare since. There is an old, double-doored metal locker propped up against the wall in the far corner. Other than that, there are several scattered crates, most of which have been broken open. There is a single door in the wall closest to you. To head for the door, turn to **305**. To check out the locker, turn to **151**. If you'd sooner take a closer look at the broken crates, turn to **300**.

268

The road here is quiet and deserted. You take a moment to enjoy the relative peace. Only the distant sounds of sirens and wailing arcades punctuate the silence. Above you, you are aware of vehicles flying through the drizzle, but the concrete walkways are so dense that they almost form a dome over the slums. It's an eerie oasis in the otherwise noisesome city. It doesn't last for long.

You follow the road as it weaves between stacked transporter units and even the odd concrete building until you see a flickering orange light ahead, hidden around a corner.

If you listen carefully, you can make out the hollow sound of chanting and shrill laughter. You glance back over your shoulder and consider heading back to the main road to check out the tram station. To retrace your steps, turn to **90**. To push on and turn the corner, turn to **95**.

269

The motor rattles into life, and the platform begins its slow crawl towards the roof of the building. As you crest the lip, you notice a group of hooded clan members gathered around a flaming metal drum. You try to press the other button, but they notice your arrival and take an immediate interest. There is no way you can fight them on the platform, so you quickly scale the lip of the building and drop onto the asphalt just in time to draw your weapon. One of them breaks rank and steps towards you, taking on the role of their leader. You can't make out their faces under their heavy hoods, but their nervous chittering tells you all you need to know. That and the fact that the others are cowering a good distance away. You get the sense that they will break and flee if you can kill one of them. These aren't

hardened clan members like you used to
be. They are probably just hangers-on,
desperate to do something to earn a place
in the clan's ranks. Whatever their cause,
your death would spell instant respect
amongst their peers.

CLAN MEMBER:

Strength: 8
Health: 8

If you defeat the clan member, the others
flee as expected. You may investigate
the rest of the roof by turning to **308**.
Otherwise, you can use the platform to
return back to the street by turning to **236**.

270

The gentle motion of the tram carriage
allows you to rest briefly, restoring *2
HEALTH POINTS*. You swiftly arrive at the
WEST STATION and disembark, darting out
into the shadows before any of the handful
of waiting commuters can notice you. You
descend the steps quickly, wincing at each
echoing clang as your heavy boots hit the
metal. A few people seem to stop and stare
in your direction, but none say anything.
You pull your hood up over your head and

sprint along the street, sticking to the single pavement and avoiding the beams of light cast by the rusting hovercabs as they ferry a trickle of passengers to and from the station.

Eventually, you emerge at a crossroads. The road to your right leads back towards the main road through the district and holds no appeal right now. Ahead of you, the road narrows swiftly into an alleyway that terminates at a high metal wall. There is a single metal hatchway cut into the wall, but from here, it is impossible to see if it is locked. To your left, the road continues in darkness for a while before stopping at the base of a squat, broken-down building. It was perhaps once built entirely of concrete, but now it is patched up with endless sheets of corrugated metal and held together by the mesh of wires that appear to have ensnared the building like vines.

To continue straight ahead into the alleyway, turn to **209**.

To turn left and head towards the building, turn to **291**.

271

You pull your weapon from your pocket and aim it squarely at the surgeon's head. She shakes her head softly and growls. Whatever upgrades she offered to you, she has clearly had something better done to herself. She flies across the room in a blur, snatches up a pulse-rifle and fires off the first round before you've even blinked. The bolt rips through your heavy coat and seers your arm. Deduct *2 HEALTH POINTS*.

BACK-ALLEY MECHIST:

Strength: 12
Health: 12

If you defeat her, turn to **265**.

272

A weak wooden door hangs loosely on old hinges at the entrance to the wooden room. You swing it open and step into a large storage cupboard. The walls are lined with warped shelves tied to rusting metal racks. You pull on a thin chain hanging just inside the door, and a weak light buzzes into life, filling the room with the speckled shadows of a thousand dead flies. Most of the shelves are empty or stacked with old pieces of mech. There are a couple of boxes of food and a tray of miscellaneous first-aid equipment. If you haven't already raided this room, you add 2 **POWERCAKE BARS** (**HEALTH +2**) and a **RESTORATE SERUM** (**HEALTH +4**) to your **PACK**.

With the room exhausted, you head back out to the main space. Turn to **31**.

273

The voice on the other side of the door sniggers, "That's not even a good pun. A real comrade would know our motto, and that certainly isn't it."

Before you can react, another hatch opens in the door, this one at waist height. A thin metal pole quickly appears through the hole and jabs you in your stomach. You recoil in pain and crash to the floor, spasming with the effects of the sudden and large jolt of flux. Deduct **2 HEALTH POINTS**. When you finally stop twitching and the smell of burnt flesh retreats, you stagger to your feet and ask for another chance.

Choose your answer.

"Rise With Pies!" - Turn to **45**.
"The Emperor Must Pie!" - Turn to **165**.

274

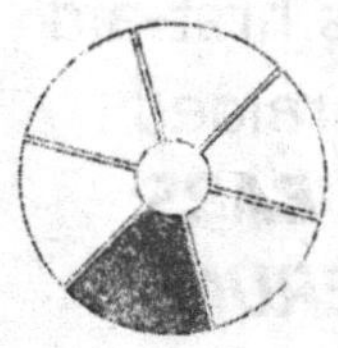

You wade through the thick sludge, knee-high in places, until you reach a shadowy area filled with soft whispers.

Turn to **321**.

275

You turn and open the door, but a thin cable flicks out of the air behind you, snatches it from your hand and slams it closed. You spin around in time to see a strange man floating down from the roof above. His face is decorated with strange red and black markings, various metal plates and wires protruding from his ruptured skin. His two eyes glow red behind a set of mirrored glasses. A separate set of black orbs blink at you from his forehead. No doubt they are fitted with some form of vision-enhancing tech. Both of his arms have been replaced with cyborg limbs powered by pistons and cogs. Chains and cables link what remains of his body to his mech limbs, while thicker wires run from his back up to the ceiling. Whilst he gives the impression of floating down towards you, the mechanical man is actually being lowered by his own life-support system.

"Leaving so soon," he hisses through pursed lips. His golden teeth blaze like fire in the glow of his eyes. "I haven't given you what you came for yet!"

"Who are you?" you cry out, desperately pulling on the door handle but getting nowhere.

"They call me the Mad Mechist," he says with a deep laugh. "They think that's an insult, but I consider it a badge of honour. Every great scientist was considered mad at some point."

You leave the door and sprint across the room to see if there is another way out. While you search, the Mad Mechist reaches the floor and begins to walk slowly towards you. His wires pull at his limbs, but he doesn't seem to notice.

"I can help you," he bellows. "I know all about Magron Thundergill. I have information that will help you. I promise that it won't hurt, and it won't cost you a ding."

If you are interested in hearing more about the mechist's offer, turn to **249**. To refuse and fight him, turn to **289**.

276

The pistol feels heavy in your hands, and your breath comes in ragged bursts. You've never been very good at the long shots; up close and personal has always been your motto. Still, you've made your choice, so you try to steady your nerves. If you are to be successful, you know that you will need to hit both guards in quick succession. From this distance, each shot will need to be a dead hit. Roll two dice. If you roll any 6s, the shot is a direct hit, and the guard slumps to the ground. If either or both are anything other than a 6, then your plasma charge fires wide of the target, and you must fight the guard up close and personal. Each has the same stats, and both must be killed before you can progress.

IMPERIALIST GUARD:

Strength: 10
Health: 8

Once both are dead, turn to **79**.

277

It takes more than a few minutes, but you gradually manage to weave your way through the grating, past the barbed wire, and drop down onto the top crate. The wood is rotten but just about manages to hold your weight. You scramble down into the dank, shadow-filled square. The walls seem to ooze damp, and green slime covers the base of the concrete walls and gives the whole yard an alien feel. Turn to **55**.

278

Thinking on your feet, you begin to lie. You mention that you may have heard a rumour about somebody called Mandrake but that you have no specific information. Perhaps they are nothing more than a myth created to give the rebels hope. You lay it on thick about how you grew up in these streets and just want to see them thriving, something that only the Emperor can achieve.

As you speak, the woman's face breaks into a soft smile, creased at the corners but warm. "And that is all you know?" she asks, stroking your cheek with a cold hand. "You see, I think that was a wonderful story

but nothing more. We know who you are
and what you are looking to do here. There
is nothing left for you here in District-U,
and yet you return? Why? You mentioned
Thundergill yourself. Revenge against him is
long overdue for you and the other rebels.
I understand. I just want to know the truth.
It's such a shame that you don't think that
we can be friends."

Stepping away from you, the woman
retreats to the mirror and presses a hidden
switch somewhere behind it. It pivots
up and disappears into the wall. You had
assumed that somebody was watching
from behind it, but instead, it was hiding
a shallow cupboard filled with a range of
equipment designed simply to inflict pain.

If you have a Silver Tongue Microchip
upgrade and you activate it successfully,
turn to **223**. Otherwise, turn to **132**.

279

The alley twists and turns but is rarely
wider than a few feet. Every few steps,
a stranger bumps into you and mutters
a hurried apology as they disappear into

the darkness. It's only after you've been harried in this way a few times that you think to check your possessions. You are immediately aware that your wallet feels thinner, and to your dismay, you realise that the pickpockets have stolen half of your money. Remove 150 **DING**. Turn to **184**.

280

The pair of 'droids look at you momentarily, waiting for you to produce a verified union card. It quickly becomes clear that you are an intruder, but the pressing line of bodies behind you makes escape impossible. You reach for a weapon, but the metallic arms of the robots grab your wrists before you make it halfway to your pack, and they wrench you off the floor, leaving your ankles dangling manically.

You scream desperately, a last-ditch attempt to draw attention to your plight, but the soulless eyes of the workers behind you stare emptily into space. They've seen it all before. Your death will mean nothing more to them than a slight delay in their passage through the gate.

Seconds fly by, and nobody comes to your aid, and your body grows weary. By the time you force yourself to calm down, the guards have dragged you to the lasergate. You can feel the pulsing heat from the beams against your skin. Luckily, the pain you feel as your body is sliced into chunks and gathered by the meat-hoarders is over swiftly, as is your life.

281

The steel clangs underfoot, a warning that you are climbing above your station. You know that if you are stopped, your citizen card won't save you up here. Without proper authorisation, you'll be sent packing in short order. Or worse.

Up here, the slums are just as rundown. The shanty buildings made from scrap metal hammered together and strapped to any available pole look just as rife with disease and misery. The people, however, are subtly different. They carry themselves with slightly more pride and purpose, their faces careworn but less so. This level is reserved for the workers in the mine, subservient and undervalued but a step above those reduced to stealing for a living. You feel the

same acid rise in your throat that you used to taste when you went to battle against these people in the distant past. The higher-ups were the enemy almost as much as the other clans. Almost, but not quite.

Up here, the cybernetics are more polished. The edges where they have been stitched to the flesh are smoother and neater. Not like the ragged wounds that the poor sods on the lowest level live with.

The same neon signs cast their flickering pools onto the wet pavement, and you set out to explore. Turn to **320**.

282

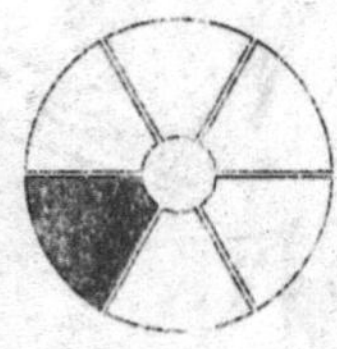

As you follow the passage, you become aware of a foul stench. Eventually, you reach a passage that opens off to your right, heading north. It is filled with foul-smelling waste but seems to be open enough for you to pass through if needed. Alternatively, you may continue west along the passage.

To continue west, turn to **294**.

To investigate the foul passage to the north, turn to **274**.

In this area of the city, most of the buildings are hab units where the workers live when they aren't busting a gut in the factory. They are small, ramshackle structures, either built from sheet metal or hollowed-out transporter silos. Thick, serpentine wires hang between them all, most of them heavy with washing that is getting wetter with every drop of filthy rain that filters down from the wealthy elite above. The smell of damp cloth is everywhere, mixing gently with the rich aromas of a galaxy's worth of local cuisine and the cloying stench of motor oil. Nobody stares at you here. These are the types of streets that raised you. Your own childhood home is long gone, but for all the ding in the world, you wouldn't be able to tell the difference between these and it.

Wandering slowly between the habs, you try to think about your next move. Somewhere in this neighbourhood, there is a MindPod with your name on it. If you can destroy that, you might finally have a shot at Thundergill.

You are snapped out of your reverie by an older woman tugging at your coat.

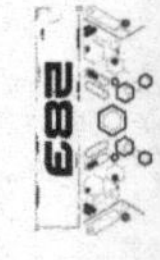

She has the well-worn but welcoming face of the street mothers that run these neighbourhoods. Respected by everyone, they roam the streets with impunity, handing out wisdom and, just like this one, food. You gratefully accept the preferred bowl of stew and eat it quickly, thanking her with a bow. The warm broth fills you up quickly, restoring *4 HEALTH POINTS*.

You soon reach a junction. To your left, the road ends quickly at a strange building. Somebody has turned several transporter units on their side and joined them with a web of scaffolding and girders. A small red door seems to be the only break in the sheet metal. To your right, the road dog legs around another set of rusting habs.

To head left, turn to **237**. To follow the road round to the right, turn to **268**.

284

You wake in a darkened room. The walls and floor are lined with once-white tiles, though they are now stained dark brown with ancient blood. A thin layer of frost has formed in places, a testament to the chilled air. Each breath hangs for a second in front of your face before drifting away. Chains hang from the walls, each one terminating in a shackle. The room itself is clinical, but the implements of torture seem rudimentary and barbaric. There's a soft hum in the air that seems to be coming from a small camera dome nestled high in the corner. A pale red light flickers; they are watching you.

Whoever tied you to the hard chair in which you find yourself knew what they were doing. You thrash against your bonds to no avail. The chair doesn't move. It's clearly bolted to the floor. Whatever is going to happen to you needs you to be securely fastened. You heard of rooms like this when you were a boy - that there were dark cells hidden under the district where dissidents and rebels would be taken to extract information. It didn't seem to matter if they talked or not. None of them ever returned. You lost more than a few friends to the shadowy guards, and you feel the bile rising in your throat at the thought of becoming another.

Somebody has noticed that you are awake

and are approaching the single door into the room. It's behind you, but there is a large, albeit tarnished, one-way mirror on the wall opposite. You calm yourself and wait for them to enter, knowing full well that they won't be here for a quiet chat.

The door slides open with a well-oiled hiss and closes just as quickly. A strange woman, dressed head to toe in a white jumpsuit, enters and stands in front of you. Her face is hard and covered with scars. Her left eye is crossed by a deep scar, the pupil pale and dilated. It's unlikely that she can still see through it, although there is always the possibility that it has been replaced with a mech upgrade.

"You're not a guard," you snap at her, once again straining against your bonds.

"And you are no street-rat rebel," she hisses. "Let's get the niceties out of the way. You are looking for Mandrake, and my master wants to know what she is up to."

"Thundergill," you snarl, his name like acid on your tongue. "What does he want?" The woman bursts into a shallow laugh.

"Magron Thundergill is nothing more than a pawn. I answer to a higher power, to the leader of all that walks or crawls in this life."

"The Emperor?" If the Emperor is aware of your existence, then there is no telling how much trouble you are in.

The woman responds with raised eyebrows and a knowing smirk. "So, what do you know?"

You swallow hard, your dry throat aching against the cold.

To lie to the woman, turn to **278**.

To tell her everything you know, turn to **10**.

285

The crowd slowly begins to clap and chant, growing louder until their electric buzz fills the square. Somebody somewhere kills the power, and the hum of the neon lights drifts away along with their light. Another switch is flicked, and a ring of low orange bulbs flickers to life around the base of the bleachers. They don't illuminate a lot, but they do cast an eerie orange glow over the grit. Underneath you, the ground shakes.

Particles of grit and sand dance over each other, and a series of small ripples spread out from a point a few feet away from you. Before you can react, the ground dips briefly before erupting into the sky. When the dust settles, you stand face to face with a thick worm, a dozen feet long and as thick as your waist. Everybody growing up in District-U knows about the sandworms; it's why you never left the walls of the city until the day you fled forever. Now, you'll have to fight your childhood nightmare.

SANDWORM:

Strength: 11
Health: 12

If you destroy the beast, turn to **314**.

286

The room you have entered is spacious and with high ceilings, but the sheer volume of bodies pressed into the space makes it feel oppressive. As you take it in, you realise that the metal beams supporting the ceiling aren't actually that far above you, but rather the whole floor has been dug out into a circular pit, giving the room

an artificial sense of height. Concrete walls line the pit, and wooden bleachers encircle the whole thing, giving the entire room the feel of an ancient colosseum. You push your way through the baying crowd until you're pressed up against the low concrete wall, looking down into the pit. A dozen feet below you, a large, muscular man, sweating and grunting with effort, it attempting to twist the head from a much smaller but evidently far stronger young woman. An enormous cheer erupts from half the crowd, echoed with an equally raucous groan from the other half, as she slips clear of his grasp, spins on one heel and plants a stiletto heel through his thigh. You wince on behalf of the fighter and watch the exchange of **DING** as one half of the crowd collects their winnings, and the other half bemoans their loss.

It is clear that you have entered a fighting pit. There is nothing to be gained from spending any more time in here watching others fight for their own glory, but should you wish to try to earn some **DING** yourself, the option to volunteer to fight is available to you.

If you wish to fight, turn to **7**.

If it's not for you and you'd sooner save your health, turn to **36**.

287

You approach the metal hatch at the end of the street, but you don't even try to unlock it. Instead, you make short work of moving the foetid trash that has piled against the fortified wall until you reveal the manhole cover. The lid comes away easily, and you are soon staring down into a dark abyss. Somebody has taken the trouble to hammer rusting pipes into the walls as a makeshift ladder, so you use these to scramble down into the darkness. Turn to **8**.

288

Halfway between the towers and the wall, your heavy boots catch on a splintered piece of metal, and you tumble to the ground. The guards surround you in seconds, drawing their electroblades and waiting to see what you do next. Turn to **152**.

The Mad Mechist hisses at you and rotates his arms. The clawed hands disappear and are replaced by a set of glowing Flux blades. When he attacks, his weapons cut away your human flesh and replace it with sheets of mech steel. His goal is simply to encase you in metal and turn you into a robotic follower of his own cult. The side effect of this is that every time you lose a round of the fight, your body becomes stronger. Increase your **STRENGTH** by +1 each time you lose, as well as removing the usual **HEALTH POINTS**. If your **HEALTH** drops below half of your maximum, turn to **27**. You may not use any mech upgrades to flee this fight as you are trapped in the building by the mechist's powers.

MAD MECHIST:

Strength: 14

Health: 14

If you defeat the Mad Mechist, turn to **92**.

You follow the dark road for a while, feeling isolated from the district only a few paces away. The sound is muffled by the towering buildings, and you are directly underneath a large factory on the level above. It's dark, and the lack of other people makes it seem even more eerie. Eventually, you reach another crossroads. To your left, the road seems to head towards another tram station, this one marked **WEST STATION**. You can think of no reason why you would need to ride another tram, so rule that out. Ahead of you, the road continues to a ramshackle building that was once solid concrete but now seems to be held together by corrugated metal sheets and the thick wires that crisscross the whole structure like vines. To your right, the road narrows into an alleyway which terminates at a fortified wall. There is a strong metal hatch in the way, but from here, you can't know if it is unlocked or not.

To press on ahead, turn to **291**.

To turn right, turn to **209**.

When you reach the small building, you notice that the door is guarded by a well-armoured woman. Before you can work out how you are going to get past her, she gives you a nod and opens the door. Confused, you step into the building.

Compared to the dark street outside, the room you enter is surprisingly well-lit. A couple of white fluorescent tubes hang from the ceiling, suspended on thin chains and bare electrical wires that crackle and buzz intermittently. A few rogues are lounging around the edges of the room, a few of them you recognise from Mandrake's hideout.

"Take a seat," one of the faceless voices in the shadows says. "Mandrake will be back soon."

You slide into a deep leather chair and gratefully place your feet up onto the broken remains of a small table. An overwhelming sense of relief washes over you, and you feel yourself begin to heal as you rest. Restore *6 HEALTH POINTS*.

While you recuperate, another stranger wanders over and introduces themself as Mandrake's personal mechist and offers to upgrade you with any mech upgrades that your heart desires, for a price, of course. She explains that her upgrades use only the very best tech parts and are guaranteed not to fail. If you choose to upgrade, you will not need to roll to use them. They will work as expected and won't fail unless something else destroys them.

NIGHT VISION

300 DING

Your night vision upgrade will allow you to see moderately better in areas where there is little light. You will be offered the option to use it if it is relevant to the situation.

PISTON LEGS

450 DING

Your piston legs will increase your speed two-fold. If you are engaged in a battle, and it isn't going your way, you can use your piston legs to flee the scene. Some battles will make it clear that you can't flee regardless of upgrades. If it doesn't mention this, then you may assume you can make a clean getaway. If you flee, follow

the instruction for successfully defeating
the enemy, but you must not claim any
WEAPONS or items that you would if you
had beaten them.

POWER GAUNTLET

500 DING

Replacing the bones in your hand with a
flexible and strong polymer and the skin
with modified sandworm hide, the power
gauntlet increases your **STRENGTH** by +2.

MECHHEART UPGRADE

600 DING (400 DING IF YOU ALREADY HAVE A MECHHEART IMPLANT):

This biotechnic heart will increase your
maximum health by +6 and restore your
health to full. If you don't already have a
MECHHEART implant, then you will also
receive a **STRENGTH** +1 upgrade.

SPIKED FEET

700 DING

A minor upgrade that places sharpened
metallic spikes into the top of each foot.
When activated during a fight, they inflict
extra damage. This upgrade will increase
your damage output from 2 points per
round to 3.

You may choose any upgrades while you wait. Once you have chosen and paid, mark them on your **MECH UPGRADES** sheet.

If you have a **SHARD OF METAL** in your **PACK**, turn to **248**.

Otherwise, turn to **295**.

292

A few women, mostly old and mostly non-human, hang out of windows on the upper floors and shriek at you in strange languages. Their message is easily recognisable: "Come and buy whatever it is I'm selling." You ignore them and push on. You discover another side street branching off to your left, but this one seems to have been barricaded off by a pile of old metal ammo crates and empty flux canisters. It seems like it would be fairly easy to climb over them if you choose to explore in that direction (turn to **161**). If not, you continue along the narrow street. Turn to **242**.

293

You cry out in pain as muscles pop all over your body, but the door won't shift.

You hear somebody on the other side but don't step out of the way in time. The door explodes inwards, smashing into you and spreading your nose across your face. You immediately taste blood and feel a warm, sticky mess drip over your lips. Stood in the doorway is a small, stooped man. His back is bent so severely that his chin almost touches the ground in front of him. His eyes are sunken in deep sockets, and they are turned upwards to stare hatefully at you. His face is a network of scars. Both of his ears have been sliced away sometime in the distant past. Turn to **12**.

294

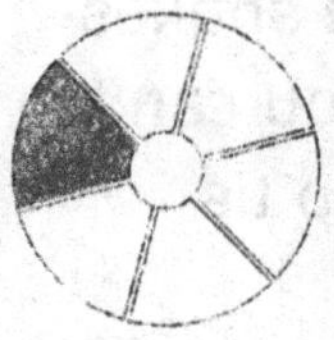

You stop at a metal hatchway in the wall. It is open, and looking inside, you see a small but dark room. You can enter the room by turning to **93**.

Alternatively, you can return the way you came by turning to **189**.

295

The warm embrace of the chair doesn't mask the cold fear gripping your chest.

When Mandrake returns, she will undoubtedly ask why you haven't destroyed the MindPod.

Sure enough, she soon bursts through the door, but she seems to be in an elated mood.

"We did it!" she shouts to the figures huddled around the walls. "We destroyed most of Thundergill's MindPods." You stand to join the celebrations, but Mandrake swiftly turns and stares you down. "What happened?" she demands.

You try to mumble some explanation about not having enough time or not knowing where it was, but your words seem empty amidst their excitement. Mandrake shakes her head and purses her lips. "If you can't do that, how can I trust you to help us further?"

You plead for another chance to prove your worth, to get revenge on Thundergill. Maybe she is just desperate for help, or perhaps Mandrake can see how sincere your hunt for vengeance is, but she gives you the slightest nod.

Turn to **88**.

296

You try to snip the wires but immediately know that you have guessed incorrectly. A strong surge of electricity grips your muscles and burns your veins as it flows through your spasming body. You shake away the pain and try to regroup for another try. The jolt of electricity causes *2 HEALTH POINTS* damage and possibly damages any mech upgrades that you have. Roll a die for each upgrade. On a 6, that upgrade is damaged beyond repair and is no longer available to you.

Return to **216** to try again.

297

The fog is beginning to thicken by the time you step back down onto the bricks. A cold chill has infiltrated the air, and the incessant rain is beginning to grate more than normal.

To look inside the "Sweeney's Pies", turn to **255**.

To work your way into the storefront marked as "Spike's Weapons", turn to **302**.

298

Half expecting the hovercab to spring to life and follow you, you try your hardest to blend into the crowd of bodies heading away from the Rusty Pipe.

The rain is now torrential and reaches even this far down into the slums. For what little protection it offers, you roll up the collar on your coat and pull your hat down tighter onto your head. All it does is create a funnel straight to your spine, but it's better than the alternative.

The flickering neon glow of the city is even brighter, reflected in the puddles that coat the pavements and roads like oil slicks. Horns blare as drivers and pedestrians fight for their own right to get home quickly while the thundering footsteps of criminals and the screams of their victims complete the musical score of your childhood.

You stop for a second and bask in the hedonistic memories of your misspent youth, but a body crashing into you brings you back to the present. Your assailant, a wiry factory worker no doubt on his way back to a small hab unit on the outskirts, apologises profusely without taking the time to stop. You wave him on his way and think about your next move.

Mandrake said that the MindPod you are to target is somewhere to the east of the city, near a tram station. You glance up at the glass tubes that crisscross the city and rattle with the occasional whoomph of air as a hovertram speeds past.

You follow the track out to the east, where you can see several stations raised on steel girders to the height of the second or third levels of the surrounding buildings. Stealing a ride on the trams was the only time you ever went that high as a kid. You don't love the idea of being trapped in the confined space of a pod, but it might be the quickest way to get to the MindPod and carry out your end of the deal.

Whatever incident had led to the main road being barricaded seems to have been cleared up. There are a few Imperialist guards still milling around questioning people, but they don't seem to have noticed you. You head along the middle of the road, ducking out of the way of a

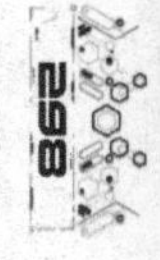

heavily-armoured convoy of slick black vehicles. They don't seem inclined to stop for anybody. Several other pedestrians are knocked out of their way in their haste to reach the factory further along the main strip.

Ignoring them, you look around. The road continues towards the flux core and the factory system. A short distance ahead, there is a set of steps leading up to a tram station. Alternatively, there is a narrower but still busy side road heading off into the east. To continue ahead, turn to **128**. To head east, turn to **283**.

299

Slowly, you return your pistol to its holster and raise your hands in surrender. The barman grunts and drops you to the floor. "It's a shame your drink spilt like that," he grumbles. "You ain't having another one."

To lean over the bar to get a closer look at the poster, turn to **245**. To leave the bar and move towards the small, quiet room, turn to **179**. If you've already investigated the other room, you return to the street. Turn to **62**.

Most of the crates are empty and heavily rotted. You make your way past them until you are brought up short by the well-rotted corpse of a young woman. She appears to have been attacked by several heavily armed assailants, judging by the deep cuts on her body. Most of her equipment seems to be undamaged. To rummage through her belongings, turn to **207**. Otherwise, you return to the main space of the warehouse floor. Turn to **185**.

As you make your way along the street, you become aware of an industrious noise coming from a squat warehouse off to your right. The windowless walls seem to be decorated with various clan tags and anarchist posters, but your attention is mainly drawn to the shuttered roller door that seems to be the only way inside. There is no signage to indicate what may lay on the other side, but it does seem to be unguarded.

To approach the door, turn to **110**.

To continue along the street, turn to **120**.

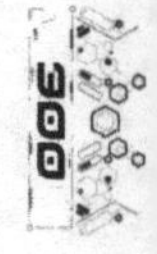

302

It doesn't take you long to break into Spike's, a simple rectangle room with a sealed door on the far side. The ashes of a fire in the middle of the floor are cold but fresh. It seems that somebody uses this room at night, and you'd rather not be here if they return. You give the room a quick scan and spot a cabinet on the far side. Your ears prick up at the sound of somebody moving about in the alleyway behind you, but you can't make out what they are saying.

To return to the alley, turn to **163**.

To look inside the cabinet, turn to **126**.

303

There seems to be nothing else of interest in the room, so you make your way to the door. Just as you are about to leave, you notice a folder on one of the tables. It is labelled with the name Magron Thundergill, so you snatch it up for a closer look. It is filled with detailed medical information, including holographic images of his body. By the looks of it, he's had a lot of mech

upgrades fitted himself, far more than most people could afford. If the information is true, then it's going to be much harder to defeat him than you expected.

"I can help you defeat him." The voice is metallic and clipped, almost robotic in nature. You spin around in time to see the body of a man hovering down from the ceiling.

Turn to **50**.

304

It doesn't take long before you are lost in the maze of alleys and streets that crisscross between the towering piles of sheet metal that the citizens of District-U call home. You wander around for a while, trying desperately to get your bearings, before you finally emerge onto what might be a main road. Turn to **5**.

305

You enter the room slowly, the door creaking ominously as you do. The hot stench from the room hits you in the nose with a physical force, sending you reeling

sideways. You blink in the acrid air, trying to make sense of the scene in front of you. Several corpses are hanging from the ceiling, flayed and partially dismembered. Huddled around a pile of meat on the floor are three of the foulest wretches you've ever seen. You've heard rumours of the meat-hoarders, a group who collect the dead bodies that mount up in a lawless dump such as District-U. If what you've heard is true, they recycle the bodies for parts at factories on the outsides of the district, and any leftover meat is used to provide food for the dregs of society who can't even afford to live in the slums. You've never believed the stories until now, but the foul evidence is clear to see.

Sensing your presence, one of the men looks up, his face richly coated in thick blood. He howls something unintelligible, and the other two beasts rise to their feet. They grab an assortment of cleavers, knives and hooks and encircle you.

The bodies and minds of meat-hoarders are twisted and warped by their diet. You must defeat all three, but before you battle each one, you must roll to determine their **STRENGTH** and **HEALTH**.

MEAT-HOARDER:

Strength: Roll a single die
Health: Roll two dice

If you defeat all three, you leave the sickening room behind. To check out the locker, turn to **151**. If you haven't looked at the broken crates and would like to, turn to **300**.

306

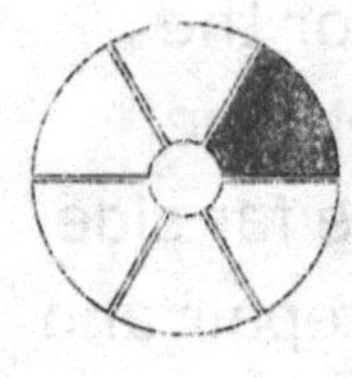

You swiftly reach the end of the passage, where it branches off to the east and west.

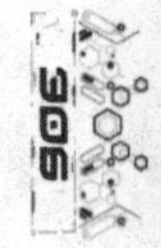

To head east, turn to **189**.

To head west, turn to **294**.

307

You fall to the ground, your face pressed into the dirt under a flurry of attacks from their metal pipes and steel-capped boots. Your bones are too broken to move, and the taste of blood is rich in your mouth.

Satisfied with your demise, the cultists return to their chanting, their low hum wafting over you along with the acrid smoke of their fire. You watch on from your lowly position as the metallic man rises from the flames once again, only this time, they continue to screech until he steps from the ashes and stands before you, a robotic giant pulsing with molten energy. The last thing you see is his plate-sized fist rushing towards your face.

308

Most of the roof is empty, except for the odd air filtration vent and Flux inlet pipe. There is a single metal crate on the far side of the roof. It looks to be in good repair and locked, but there might be a way to get in.
Turn to **127** to head over to investigate.
Turn to **236** to return to the street.

309

As you expect, the others flee before their leader hits the floor. That won't be the last of the Jongleurs, and they'll have you marked for death now. You would do well to try to avoid them in future if at all possible.

You step over the multi-coloured corpse and continue into the maze of streets. Eventually, you emerge onto a wider road that seems to serve as a main thoroughfare for the district. Turn to **5**.

310

You push the man away from you and swing the brick in a perfect arc. It cracks into the side of his head with a sickening thud. He drops to the floor, unmoving. You don't have time to check on him. You simply head for the open door. The brick will make a suitable weapon for now, so your **STRENGTH** is restored to your basic level. Turn to **145**.

311

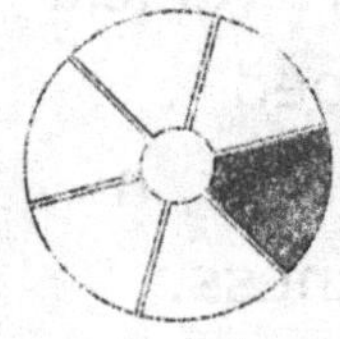

You follow the wooden pathway due east. After a while, you spot an opening on your left, heading north. There is a small gap between the wooden walkway, which continues east, and a muddy embankment to the north. You can't see on the other side of the small pile of sludge, but the toxic effluence doesn't seem to be flowing through the mound.

To make the jump and head north, turn to
73.

To push on east, following the wooden
walkway, turn to **183**.

312

You twist the final wire into place and wait
for anything to happen. For a second,
nothing seems to change inside the
MindPod, but then the whole unit begins to
emit a deep hum and starts to vibrate and
groan. Within seconds, it is shaking on its
foundations, the metal beginning to glow
red with the heat being generated inside.
You glance around for somewhere to hide,
but the only way out is an even narrower
alleyway. You squeeze between the walls
and dive behind a burnout transport vehicle
just as the world around you is ripped
apart in a pulsing torrent of green light, a
powerful shockwave and then darkness.

Turn to **204**.

313

Something about the building has drawn
you in, but you don't want to risk getting

into a fight with the guard. Still, the other distractions along the street offer nothing to you now, and you hastily make your way back to the small square and the steps up to the tram station. If, as you suspect, the tram carriage you saw really was connected to the building, then perhaps that will provide you with a way inside. You leap into the first carriage that arrives, pushing aside a waiting patron, and glance at the glowing buttons.

Choose your destination:

EAST STATION (Turn to **160**)

WEST STATION (Turn to **270**)

CENTRAL LOWER STATION (Turn to **164**)

314

A hideous groan escapes the monster's foul mouth as you fire the final plasma pellet into its gut. It crashes to the ground, and the crowd erupts into a cacophony of cheers and thunderous applause. You don't kid yourself; their celebrations would have been just as joyous had you lost. All they wanted to see was a fight. A small man wanders over to you. His back is hunched, but his left eye sparkles with the mechanical glow of a cybernetic eye. Only its owner will know the benefits that it bestows upon him, but these modifications are no longer the trademark of the rich or those in a clan. He looks up at you with a mirthless smile and pressed a handful of notes into your hand. "Get out of here," he says gruffly. "There's more where that thing came from."

Add 300 **DING** to your **PACK** and turn to **9**.

315

The **PERSPEX DRIVE** feels fragile in your hand and strangely futuristic compared to the complicated and archaic machine in front of you. You slide the drive into the only slot that seems to fit and wait. For a moment, nothing happens. Just as you are about to yank it back out, a small window pops up on the screen, and a long series of obscure filenames flashes past quicker than you can read them. Whatever is happening seems to have been pre-programmed by Henry.

As soon as the files have finished copying

onto the drive, it begins to flash rapidly with a pulsing green light. It emits a strange humming sound, varying in pitch from low to high, before falling silent. It seems that the device is somehow connected to the old man's system, and the files are being automatically sent to him. A few seconds later, your visual **HUD** illuminates, and a message floats across your right eye.

"Thanks for that! Here's something for your trouble." As you watch, 1000 **DING** appear in your bank account. Add them to your **PACK**.

With nothing else to catch your attention in the room, you return to the alleyway. Turn to **297**.

316

Despite your best efforts to charm him, you are met with nothing but a stern growl from the barman. "If you keep asking those sorts of questions around here, you ain't gonna like the answers," he snaps before turning away to serve another customer. You cut your losses and head towards the small room on the other side of the building. Turn to **179**.

"Take a seat." The voice is filled with nervous energy and is tinny due to the low quality and poor repair of the tannoy system, but it's clear enough for you to hear. You follow the instruction and sit on the only seat in the room, an uncomfortable metal stool bolted to the floor. After a while, your back begins to ache, and you take to pacing from corner to corner. You are certain that this is the right place, but you are growing quickly uneasy at how long it is taking for them to talk to you.

The door through to the next room is metal and in good repair. There's no way you can break it down, but it might be possible to knock on it to get their attention. It is larger than most and studded with thick rivets. There's a small metallic platform on the floor, almost like a welcome mat. It is rusting in places and bordered with striped yellow and black hazard tape that's peeling off at the corners.

Around the room, there are several cameras hanging from the ceiling and another above the door. They don't move, but you've no doubt that you are being watched at every moment.

If you decide to try hammering on the door to get their attention, turn to **22**. If you'd sooner be patient and wait, turn to **26**.

318

You try to get a good look at the strange entity, trying to decide if it's a friend or foe. As you edge closer, you feel your arms and legs stiffen and freeze, paralyzing you to the spot. You can't make out a face on the creature. The head is hooded in a thick robe that wraps around the body, disguising any form beneath it. You try to wrench your limbs free but quickly realise that they aren't being held by anything other than your own mind - something is controlling your thoughts. You stare at the being and realise that you can just make out a pair of mad yellow eyes underneath the hood and that this is one of the espers that Mandrake warned you about.

It takes all of your mental might, but you manage to force it from your head for long enough to regain your composure and grab a weapon. When fighting an esper, they are able to read your thoughts before you even act. Your chances of hitting them are greatly reduced, so you must deduct -2 from any roll you make for your own **STRENGTH** during the battle.

If you wish to force your way past the esper and flee back into the alleyway, you may attempt to do so at any point. Roll a die. On a 4-6, you overcome the mind-melding powers of the esper and flee successfully into the other passage. Turn to **130**. On a roll of 1-3, the esper lashes out with its mind and forces your limbs to stretch and bend in unnatural ways. You manage to break free, but not before the damage has been done. Deduct **2 HEALTH POINTS** before fleeing into the passage if you are still alive. Turn to **130**.

ESPER:
Strength: 10
Health: 5

If you defeat the esper, return to the main passage by turning to **130**.

319

You glance inside the room and see a heavy piece of weaponry resting against the far wall. From where you are standing, it looks like a ***NECTROTIC FLUX CANON***. They use a modified mixture of flux energy and irradiated waste to produce a chemical that strips the flesh from the bones of anything hit by it. You've heard about them, everybody has, but nobody you know has ever seen one.

The room itself is small, and the floor looks rotten. Even from the doorway, you can feel a draft floating up through the gaps.

You can enter the room to pick up the canon by turning to **247**.

If you'd sooner leave it alone and continue further along the walkway, turn to **264**.

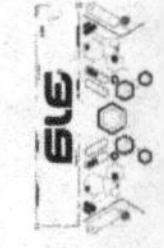

320

The metal walkway continues for miles, sprawling out in every direction, almost, but not quite, mirroring the concrete below. Every now and then, it shudders as a bullet tram flies past on the magnetic lines. There are stations on every level, but those at the bottom could never afford the fare. You remember riding it once when you were very young and the feeling of being almost weightless as it whipped you to another station. *No time for that now,* you think. Mandrake is waiting for you somewhere in the hive, and he won't wait forever.

You turn back to the steps just as a shadowy figure detaches itself from an umbrella and offers you its hand. "You don't belong up here, do you?" they say.

To listen to what they say, turn to **232**.

To push past them and return to the steps, turn to **253**.

321

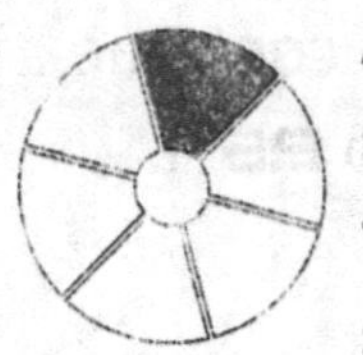As you approach the shadows, something hideous emerges from the toxic waste. An enormous skeletal beast, a dozen feet tall and covered with a thick carapace, rises over you. Its head is a disfigured orb punctured with eyes and mouths, its arms nothing more than tendrils flanked with fins like a fish. Three legs protrude from its lower body, each one a sharp talon covered

in thick armoured scales. As you howl in fear, a nest of tendrils branches out from an orifice in its chest, yanking your weapon from your hands. Whichever weapon you used last is now lost. Remove it from your **WEAPONS**.

The size of the creature means that there is no escape. Your only way forwards is to slaughter it.

SEWER DEMON:
Strength: 18
Health: 12

Upon your final blow, the demon shudders and lies still. Its enormous bulk blocks the passage to the west, so your only way out is to head east, rejoining the wooden walkway. If you'd like to pick over the demon's corpse, turn to **203**.

To leave the corpse and return to the walkway, turn to **183**.

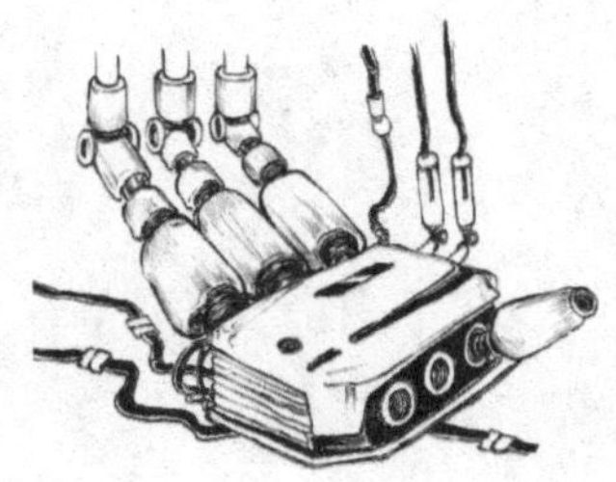

322

Your skeleton will be infused with a strange metallic fluid that bonds with your bones and makes them unbreakable. You can still be killed - after all, your flesh and organs are still only human - but your **STRENGTH** will be boosted by +4 whenever you engage your skeleton. Its power is controllable; bodies that use this power too much have a tendency to seize up, leaving the owner frozen in their own personal hell. Choose whenever you wish to implement this upgrade. Once you disengage it, your strength reduces back to normal until next time.

Turn to **83**.

THE FIGHTING PIT
WHO WILL YOU FIGHT?

D6	ENEMY	STRENGTH	HEALTH
1	Battle Droid	7	8
2	Street Brawler	9	10
3	Virulant	8	6
4	Imperialist Guard	12	9
5	Jongleur Clan Member	9	10
6	Cyborg Mech Warrior	14	12

IF YOU LOVE FANTASY...

If you love well-crafted worlds and epic fantasy adventures, you will enjoy Matt Beighton's Shadowland Chronicles.

When Trixie Grimble finds herself trapped on a distant world and embroiled in the middle of a dark and ancient war, she has to decide what she is prepared to do to make it back home.

Available online and at all good bookstores.

YOUR ADVENTURE ISN'T OVER YET...

Travel through space and time with the rest of the **Pick Your Path Adventures**, available online and to order through all good bookstores, or grab a signed copy from mattbeighton.co.uk/shop

Also available as interactive ebooks!

ABOUT THE AUTHOR

Matt Beighton is a full-time writer, born somewhere in the midlands in England during the heady days of the 1980s. He is happily married with two young daughters who keep him very busy and suffer through the endless early drafts of his stories.

Matt's books have been read around the world and awarded the LoveReading4Kids "Indie Books We Love" and Readers' Favorite 5 Star Awards.

Having spent many years as a primary-school teacher, Matt Beighton knows how to bring stories to life. He regularly visits schools and runs creative workshops that ignite a passion for words.

If you have enjoyed reading this book, please leave a review online. Your words really do keep us going!

To find out more visit

www.mattbeighton.co.uk